Mustang Round-Up

By the same author

Buckmaster
Buckmaster and the Cattlelifters
Mojave Wipeout
Buscadero
Miserywhip's Last Stand
A Devil Called Clegg
Santosbrazzi Killer
Tumbleweed
Devil's Spawn
The Undertaker
Fyngal's Gold
Night Stalker
Bareknuckle Fighter
The Chiseller
The Coffin Filler
The Grandstanders
Breakout

Mustang Round-Up

TEX LARRIGAN

ROBERT HALE · LONDON

First published in Great Britain 2000

ISBN 0 7090 6465 9

Robert Hale Limited
Clerkenwell House
Clerkenwell Green
London EC1R 0HT

Typeset by
Derek Doyle & Associates, Liverpool.
Printed and bound in Great Britain by
WBC Book Manufacturers Limited, Bridgend

One

The drumming of hooves became louder by the minute. Elijah Joe cocked an experienced ear to the sound. The palomino throwback's harem was sure in a panic. Elijah Joe wondered what had caused the small herd to stampede.

He got up from his cooking fire, shambled to his look-out and gazed down the valley. The wild mustangs usually grazed for half a day before leisurely moving. Now they were in full gallop and passing below where he had his soddy, the oldest and most important mare of the group leading the younger mares and foals with the half-grown colts on either flank and old Palo, the stallion, taking up the rear, chivvying the stragglers forward.

Far behind, as Elijah Joe shaded his eyes against the glare of the sun, he saw a long line of riders coming hell-bent behind.

He swore. The bronc-busters were at it again! Then he grinned. They would never catch up with old Palo's herd of wild mustangs, not unless one of the young ones stumbled and fell and the herd stopped to defend it.

Then there would be trouble.

Old Elijah Joe took special interest in Palo and his herd. Palo looked like palomino, with his satiny golden-brown coat, cream mane and tail and had very little sign of any other breed in him. He was a mustang all right. He had the mustang's toughness, his climbing ability and he could fight any contesting stallion that had designs on his mares.

There were black, dun and brown foals in the small group, but now and again a foal was born that had all the traits of his father.

Elijah was waiting for the day when a foal was born exactly like his father. That would be when Elijah would pounce. He wanted a son of Palo. He would be worth a fortune.

He took a poor view of the bronc-busters. They had been harrying all the herds running wild in the Montana mountains, making the animals edgy. Even Palo's herd were twitchy when Elijah Joe rode too close, and he'd been cultivating them for years. They were his only contact with a world he didn't want to know.

Now the bastards down there were stirring up trouble. If they weren't careful they would drive Palo and his herd away altogether and Elijah Joe would have to leave his comfortable soddy dug into the hillside and follow them if he ever wanted to realize his dream.

Elijah Joe hated all men. He was a lonely creature himself, more animal than human. He liked his own company. He only trusted himself. Captured by Indians when a baby, he never knew his real parents. He supposed that the Indians who brought him up had killed them. They'd treated him as a slave from the time he could gather wood for cooking-fires. But they'd taught him to survive. They'd made him clean the guts out of carcasses that had been brought home by the hunters. Later, when he was older and stronger, they'd shown him how to cut up joints of meat and how to dry strips of meat for jerky. He could make pemmican, after watching the women preparing this food for winter.

The women also showed him where to find edible roots and pointed out which were poisonous. He knew all about herbs and where to find wild garlic and where the honey-bees built their nests.

Oh, he could live off the land and did. He feasted on fish from the mountain streams and laid traps for jack-rabbits and when possible shot an occasional deer. He would lie in wait for a lame animal or an old one. He called it culling. Better be killed with one clean shot than let the animal be taken by a mountain cat.

But the great hatred in him for white people had started when he was rescued just before he came to manhood by a preacher who'd called him Elijah Joe. He'd set about turning him into a Christian by beating the hell out of him, because Elijah Joe confessed to worshipping Manitou, the Great Spirit of the Universe.

Elijah Joe never forgot that preacher. Now, as an old man he considered all white men to be as bigoted as that white-haired god-man who preached about Jesus's love for all men, and yet beat the shit out of unbelievers.

Ever since Elijah Joe, bleeding from a particularly savage attack, had shot the preacher and made for the mountains, he had kept well away from white folk, and still, after all these years, only visited the small town of Carson's Bluff to buy ammunition, coffee and flour and sugar and beans and a few tins of peaches as a luxury and to trade in his skins for same. He did this twice a year and endured the suspicious looks of those on the street as he rode in on his old mare followed by his pack mule.

He caught women glancing at him, noses sniffing, and he would look away. Women made him feel uncomfortable.

The only experience he had of women was the vague remembrance of the Indian women and girls, and of one girl in particular, Little Flower, who'd caught him bathing in the stream behind the tepees, and who'd shown him that his prick wasn't just to pee out of.

Sometimes he still dreamed about her even after all these years and it was always the same. He had wet breeches in the morning.

Now he grabbed for his rifle and, leaning on a

rock beside his look-out, he carefully drew a bead on the leading horseman. He waited until he could be sure of his shot, then muttering under his breath, 'That'll teach you to come and upset my mustangs!' He fired a shot. He felt the rifle jump, heard the explosion and the whine of the bullet as it sped on its way becoming fainter in the distance.

He watched and smiled as man and horse tumbled to the ground, then the horse righted itself and galloped away. Elijah Joe was pleased that the horse appeared to be OK. He was more interested in the still figure sprawled on the ground and the rest of the men who were pulling up abruptly and crowding around their leader.

He saw the faces looking up, scanning the mountain range, looking for clues as to where the shot came from. In the meanwhile, Palo's lead mare had turned up a narrow draw and the small herd was fast disappearing amongst the rocks and scrub.

Elijah Joe grinned to himself.

'That'll show the bastards they can't just ride into the wild country and capture as many mustangs as they see fit, God damn!'

He went back to his fire which fortunately was just glowing embers. A wisp of smoke would have given his camp away. He stirred the glowing charcoal and settled his blackened coffee-pot to heat up the brew.

He would have a snort of his home-brewed pulque to celebrate. Another little victory against the so-called civilized white men!

A rhythmic thumping of a tail roused him. The young wolf he'd saved as a pup from a trap came to him on his belly, front paws moving forward bit by bit. He grovelled, teeth bared in a grimace. The randy sod had been away for three days. He'd smelled a female in heat. Now, he was back and looking the worse for wear. There were two bites on his head, his throat was ripped, and an open wound on his flank still bled.

Elijah Joe held out a dirty hand and the wolf licked it.

'So you've had to fight for what you wanted, you randy varmint. Come here while I look you over.'

Trapper, the name the two-legged one called him, knew by the tone of voice that he was welcome. He came and rolled over onto his back to have his belly rubbed, but he yelped as the man's fingers probed his wounds, then he yelled wildly as Elijah Joe poured some of his precious pulque over the worst of the wounds.

He tried to get away, and snapped at the imprisoning fingers and got a cuff across the head for doing so.

'Stop it, you wild varmint! If you will take on those brothers of yours to get your end away, then you'll have to take the consequences. Lie still!' Trapper lay still but whined now and again until Elijah Joe finished cleaning the wounds.

Then, bounding up, he shook himself and

danced around Elijah Joe who smiled and shook his head.

'When will you learn, Trapper? Females are just trouble.' He threw him a chunk of meat. Trapper gorged himself and then lay down at his feet.

Both of them felt easy and comfortable, touching each other.

TWO

Hank Bodell groaned. He was flat on his back with a pounding head and a stinging pain in his right thigh. He blinked as his fingers sought and found the wound. His fingers came away sticky with blood . . . his blood. Goddammit! What had happened? He opened his eyes and saw some of his men looking down at him.

'Wha . . . what happened?' he managed to stutter.

'Take it easy, boss. You took a tumble.' Ned, one of his bronc-busters knelt beside him, trying to stem the blood with his bandanna. You've been lucky. The leg's only grazed.'

Jesus! Did any of you see where the bullet came from?' Hank was struggling to sit up and lean back on his elbows as Ned made a rough bandage about the damaged thigh after cutting away the canvas pants.

Ned shook his head.

'There was only the one bullet and it sounded as

if it come from a Spencer repeater. It was a good shot. Another inch to the side and it would have caught you in the chest.'

Just then Hank's partner, Linx Firman rode up with Hank's horse, which had bolted, on a loose rein. He slid lightly from his own horse, throwing both sets of reins to one of the cowboys standing around.

'Watch the horses, Abe,' he said, and strode across to where Hank was lying.

'You OK, Hank?'

'I'll live,' growled Hank. 'If I catch the bastard who did this, I'll hang him!'

Linx nodded.

'Blackie has a bullet furrow down the right side of his neck. If he hadn't deflected it, you'd be dead! It came from high up. In those hills I reckon.'

The bunch of bronc-busters looked up into the hills, but there was no sign, no disturbance, no tell-tale fire.

'It looks as if someone didn't like us going for that herd we were chasing,' Ned said slowly.

'Well, we've lost them for sure,' Hank Bodell said testily. 'I would have liked to collar that palomino. If someone can hoist me on to my horse, we'll go back to the camp.'

There was a bit of grumbling from the men. They'd chased that small herd for hours with nothing to show for it. There'd been several good yearlings amongst the group as well as the gold and cream stallion that had stood out from the rest. Also the mares looked to be in good condition. Still, you win some, you lose some. The men were used to setbacks. It was no easy job for fainthearts, for those who deliberately went out to capture and rope the wild mustangs that roamed by the thousands in Montana and Wyoming.

Back at camp, Hank had his leg cleaned and rebandaged. It would be sore for a few days but it wouldn't stop him riding. Old Jake, the cook, was a good hand with bullet wounds and the many accidents the men suffered from kicking animals and being flung from horseback during the cutting out of mustangs on the run. Sprains, and broken legs and dislocated shoulders were all in the day's work for Jake, who always offered a full whiskey bottle to any of his patients before beginning his ministrations.

Few of the men grumbled at his rough and ready methods. It was either Jake or nobody. They chose Jake.

Night came down swiftly. The cook-fire showed up cheerfully and one of the boys pulled out his mouth-organ and soon the men, replete with Jake's plain but filling grub, were ready for their nightly singaround.

Hank encouraged this. It kept the boys cheerful. He encouraged a few drinks too. That way they didn't hanker after going into the nearest town looking for women. It also meant clear heads next day, not hungover would-be stallions who'd locked horns with the local men for their women.

Any persistent drunk or fighter or womanizer was out. Hank Bodell ruled a tight crew who knew that each day of the hunting season counted. They would earn good bonuses at the end of the hunt if they stuck to Hank's strict rules.

Already they had taken more than a hundred two- and three-year-old mustangs and shipped them out. Hank had sold them on to the ranchers needing new horses. The best were kept back for the army who were always on the look-out for good mares to breed from. Hank had a standing contract with the army to take all likely stock.

On his own ranch in Wyoming, down by the Powder River, he had a growing herd of good stock, all broken in by some of the best horse-breakers in the West. These horses were the élite of all Hank's years of toil. The palomino stallion with its golden coat and fine cream mane and tail would have been the crowning glory of them all.

Hank cursed his luck. So near and yet so far. To have nearly captured that king of stallions! To have seen his beauty, the way he moved, all rippling muscle and sinew, the way he flung his proud head and marshalled his harem before him in a protective pincer movement, ready to tear and rend anyone coming too near.

Goddammit! He'd search those hills, draw by draw, and gully by gully until he found the bastard who shot him down! And when he did . . . God help him!

When the singing was over, and the men were ready to shake down he sat up and made his announcement.

'Listen, fellers, we're going after that sonofabitch with the rifle. He's probably some trapper or prospector. We're gonna round him up and have us a lynching party.' He looked round at them all in the light of the dying fire, his face twisted with hate and anger. 'What d'you say?'

Linx Firman shrugged and rubbed a stubbled chin, his dark eyes narrowed.

'We're out here to catch hosses, Hank, not waste time looking for a man who's probably long gone. It's tough on you, but we've always kept to rules, so forget it, Hank.' Linx spat into the fire. It sizzled.

Hank looked angry. He didn't expect his partner to object.

'What about you fellers?'

Ned and Abe, who were older than the other three young cowboys, shook their heads while the youngsters looked interested. Anything for a bit of excitement.

Ned rolled a cigarette before answering.

'You're lucky to be alive. The feller's a good shot even from a distance. I reckon we should just leave this area alone.'

'But I want that palomino!'

'You'll get it in time. The herds always move on. They don't stay put. We'll catch him in some other territory. No need to get any of us killed because of him.'

'Aw, come on, Ned, there's plenty of us to take him,' young Ed Gittens chirped up.

'Yes, we'll go with you, boss,' another eager young buck offered. Charlie Nelson was known to be a hothead and loved nothing better than a scrap. Ned and Abe had been astonished that he'd lasted so long with the group.

Linx Firman stood up, ready to turn in.

'Look, Hank, leave it until morning and you might think differently. I'll tell you now, I'm going hunting mustangs!'

'It's all right for you, Linx. You didn't get shot without warning! I did!' Linx shrugged and turned away.

'Wake me at sun-up, Jake, and we'll be on our way.'

When Jake awakened he scratched his belly before rising to kick the embers of the fire into a blaze. He saw at once that some of the crew were missing. He cursed. The boss was sure loco. Taking off with the youngsters, Ed Gittens and that hothead, Charlie Nelson and the Irish bog-trotter, Paddy O'Rourke.

Hastily he waddled over to where Linx Firman was curled up under a blanket and shook him by the shoulder. 'Linx, wakey-wakey.'

Linx groaned and opened his eyes at the grey dawn. 'Oh, hell. . . .'

'Wake up, Linx. The boss and the young 'uns have gone!'

Linx sat up with a jerk, now wide awake. 'Like hell they have?'

'Yeh, looks as if they slipped their bridles during the night. What shall we do, Linx?'

'Nothing, you fat sonofabitch! If Hank wants to get himself lost in these mountains, its his business. Just you get breakfast.'

Linx was furious. It was the first time in a long partnership that Hank and he had disagreed. What made it worse was the fact that he had taken with him the three young cowboys who were needed for the successful tailing and capturing of the mustangs. He and Abe and Ned wouldn't have a cat in hell's chance of catching even one spirited horse, never mind several. It needed two flankers running at the side of the fleeing herds to keep them in line, while two remained at the rear to drive the stragglers into the fold. Two others were needed to control and guide the leading mare. This was usually done by a pincer movement, panicking the mare to run in whichever direction was needed.

It was a skilful job, chasing down these wild herds. They could be guided into a box canyon and then imprisoned behind a hastily erected fence made of brush. Sometimes a basket-like barricade could be made in advance if the willow wands were available. It always depended on the terrain.

But how the hell could three middle-aged men tackle high-spirited panicky animals? Linx looked at Jake and at his paunch. It was no use considering Jake. It was years since he'd been on a round-up. He would have a heart attack and snuff it and then they'd be up shit creek without a cook, and worse, they'd have no doc.

'God damn it to hell!' he raved, as he drank hot bitter coffee and spooned up beans. 'I'll give that bastard a piece of my mind when he comes back!'

'If he comes back,' Ned said chewing on some cold belly pork.

'What d'you mean, if?' Linx's eyes narrowed. 'You know something I don't?'

Ned shrugged. 'I been in this country before. There's mountain men up there who're more vicious than the Indians. If that shootist was one of them, there might be others with him. They know the country, Hank doesn't. He could be running into trouble.'

Linx frowned. He hadn't thought of anyone else. He'd thought of one lone man out there, but now he began to worry. It was all very well being angry with Hank, but he sure didn't want anything to happen to him.

'You think we should go after him?'

'Well, we can't hunt mustangs, so we might as well take up his trail. He might need us.'

Linx nodded. Ned was talking sense. He looked at the silent Abe. 'What d'you think?'

'I think like Ned. Whoever he was, he could shoot, and a man who can shoot the distance he shot, and hit, is some dangerous feller. I think we should go after them.'

Linx looked at Jake.

'You all right on your own, or d'you want one of us to stay with you?'

Jake shook his battered frying pan. 'Who'll want to take a potshot at me? If anyone comes too close I'll brain him with this here pan!'

'Very well. You stay here until tomorrow and if we don't come back, pack up and hightail it back to Carson's Bluff.'

Sarah Crayshaw looked at her pa, a frown creasing her forehead.

'Are you sure we're on the right track, Pa? We seem to be climbing higher and higher. I thought a pass meant we could take a short cut through the mountains, a gap like.'

The four horses were struggling as they pulled the heavy wagon up the steep incline. Sarah leaned out of the wagon and looked back at Billie Devonport who was driving the second wagon. He too looked troubled. Tot Crayshaw patted his daughter's arm as he urged on the tiring beasts.

'Don't fret, love. I'm following the map that feller

drew for us. We must be somewhere close. Another few miles. . . .'

'But shouldn't we be going down, Pa? We seem to be going up the mountain for ever.'

Tot Crayshaw was beginning to worry but he didn't want his daughter to know it. Now she was irritating him with her constant fretting.

'Haven't I told you? We're on the right track! Just have patience, Sarah. That feller knew the terrain, we don't. Just trust a little, will you?'

'I didn't like the look of him, Pa, and he laughed when he gave you the map. It was as if it was some joke . . .'

'He was just a rough trapper come in for supplies. Believe me, we were lucky to find a man who knew his way over these damned mountains!'

'I still don't like it!'

'Then get down and walk awhile or get up beside Billie and leave me in peace! Women!' he muttered to himself as she jumped down, ran back to Billie's wagon and climbed up beside him.

Tot smiled to himself. Those two would make a good pair. Billie was a good hard worker and not inclined to drink. He'd be an asset when they reached his brother's ranch in Wyoming.

Tom Crayshaw had forever been on to his brother to leave the small dirt farm in Ontario and join him in Wyoming. His ranch was big enough for the two brothers to work together. A bad year for crops and the loss of Annie, Tot's wife, had decided

Tot to pack up, sell his place and join his brother. It was time for families to stick together. If anything happened to him he wanted Sarah to be with her own kinfolk.

He also wanted somewhere good for her to settle down with Billie and raise some kids. It would be right fine to be with his brother and watch his grandkids grow up. . . . He smiled at the secret dream and touched the lead horse with the whip.

'Hiyah!' he called and felt the two lead horses start to pull. Suddenly a bullet whizzed past his head. Startled, he lost the reins and the horses yawed as another bullet crashed into Tot Crayshaw's skull.

He never heard Sarah scream or saw Billie Devonport topple off his wagon and slide into the undergrowth.

Sarah, her eyes wide with horror, saw the same man who'd given her father the map, laughing up at her. He was a big man, with wide shoulders and a paunch and a grizzly beard that would have made a good nesting site for a bird. He was laughing, his thick red lips drawn back like a wolf's.

'So, the plan worked! You're just what we're looking for m'dear. Now if you'll just climb down from that wagon I'll take you to our camp.'

He put out a hand to help her down. She shrank away.

'Keep away from me, you murderer!' she spat at him.

'That's not the way to talk to someone who could protect you from . . .' he looked meaningfully towards the other men now busy looting the other wagon. 'They might get ideas, y'know.'

'Please, just leave me alone.' Sarah's voice broke. 'I want to go to my father.'

The big man looked at her and grinned.

'He's dead. No good worrying about him, so you'd best to come quietly.' Then his face changed. 'Were you driving the team or was there someone else?' He scowled now, sending frissons of fear up and down Sarah's spine.

'No . . . no . . . I was driving. Pa said I was good at it,' she lied.

'What happened to the boy who was with your pa when I gave him the map? He was in the store with him, humping sacks.'

'He was just a clerk from the store.' Sarah thanked God that Billie had let her take thc reins when he'd climbed into the back of the wagon to find the canteen of water. She hoped and prayed that he wouldn't try anything rash and get himself killed. It was Billie's escape that was now sustaining her.

There was a sudden crash as the first wagon, now empty of its load was sent careering down the mountainside to break up into broken planks and buckled wheels.

The big man watched with approval as the four wagon horses were loaded up like pack mules.

'Just take what we can pack out, boys, and when you're ready you can start on this lot!' With a quick lunge he caught Sarah by the arm and yanked her off her seat. She struggled but his meaty fists were too much for her. She was like a young doe caught in the claws of a mountain lion.

He held her like a baby and the more she struggled the more amused he was.

She watched the other men turn out the rest of their possessions and it hurt to watch a dirty youth poring over the picture of her mother and father, he standing stiffly with his hat in his hand and she sat on a carved chair and both looking very self-conscious for the photographer. Then, laughing, the youth tossed it into a crevice and turned out her father's wooden box of mementoes of a lifetime with a loving wife.

The men found her father's store of whiskey that he'd been saving for emergencies. They pulled the corks on two bottles and passed them round, growing rowdier as the bottles emptied.

Eventually they all came to stand and look at her, their lips moving suggestively. They made lewd comments and touched her and one youth tried to put a hand down her tight bodice.

She spat at him and he scowled and drew back wiping his cheek.

'You'll be sorry for that when we get back to camp,' he growled and slapped her face, knocking her to the ground. The other men laughed until

Big Barnaby intervened.

'Stop it, Zac! Don't spoil the goods before we've held an auction for her! Don't forget I was the one who spotted them and gave them the map! I have first pick!'

'It's always the same, Barnaby, you always have first go. It's not fair!'

Barnaby's answer was to knock the complaining youth down, knocking out a tooth.

The man scrambled to his feet, dabbing at his bloody mouth. 'Why, you big ape. . . .' Head down, he charged Barnaby to head-butt him. Barnaby stepped aside, his rumbling laughter like the growl of a wild beast, and lifting his foot, gave the youth a mighty kick on his backside which sent him careering into the side of the wagon. There was a sickening crash and the dazed man slid down on to the ground.

'Anybody else feel like questioning my right to have this woman first?'

The other men remained silent and one of them leaped up into the wagon and started tossing out the rest of the Crayshaw possessions. Suddenly he gave a great whoop of delight and stood balancing a strong-box on the driving seat.

'Hey! Look what I've found! We're in luck! I bet the old devil's cash is in this box!' Without more ado, he shot the padlock off.

He opened the lid. A gust of wind lifted a pile of loose paper and the breeze wafted it away. Sarah watched all her father's hard-earned cash and the money he'd got for the farm blown away like leaves in the Fall.

Barnaby cursed and raced around trying to capture some of the dollar bills, the rest of the men doing likewise. But what they saved was nothing like what had been in the chest.

There was also a bag of gold eagles, which Barnaby tucked away inside his deerskin jerkin.

'You stupid dumbhead! You should have waited until we got back to camp! We've lost a fortune through you, you bastard!'

But the incident had taken their minds off Sarah. They had someone else to resent besides Barnaby, who always expected any perks that were going.

Back at their camp, which was tucked away in a valley high up in the mountains just below the snow-line, Sarah saw a cluster of shacks, a number of men and a few silent women watching the little cavalcade coming in.

The women's eyes flashed at the thought of booty. Maybe there would be some household utensils, soap and clothes.They looked at Sarah like vultures, assessing her size, her appearance and how long would she be of interest to Barnaby.

They were scrawny sullen women, unable to meet Sarah's frightened eyes. Some turned away. Others looked at her boldly, consideringly, but none with pity.

They too had undergone the trauma of being

captured and brought to this place. They had survived, so would she.

The men threw the bundles and the boxes on to the ground and watched the women fight over Sarah's and her father's possessions. Barnaby took care of the bag of gold pieces and the bundle of dollar bills he had gathered up. He was still in a rage at the man who'd shot the padlock off the box. He would deal with the fool later.

He laughed as he watched the women fight each other for Sarah's underwear and her few pitiful skirts and blouses. Several of the women stripped off their rags and paraded in the items they'd grabbed. Two or three small children stood wide-eyed with fingers in mouth at the spectacle of their mothers clawing each other to lay claim to pots and pans and Sarah's mother's beloved kitchen scales.

Then she was being rudely dragged from the horse she'd been thrown upon like a sack of corn, and Barnaby took her into a dark ill-smelling den that was half log cabin and half cave, dug right back into the hillside. It smelled of damp, stale liquor and unwashed bodies. There was no window and light came through the cracks of the rough wooden door.

'You settle yorself, m'dear, while I go sort these here hardcases out. Those women are goin' to kill each other if somethin' ain't done. You and I have plenty of time to get to know each other!' He laughed in an unpleasantly suggestive way. He slammed the door behind him and Sarah heard the heavy wooden plank drop into place on the outside.

The light came through the rough planks like tiger stripes and she felt around and saw that besides a rough table and a couple of benches there was only a rickety bed covered by a mangy bearskin. She shuddered. The smell was now appalling and most of it seemed to be coming from the bed.

Apart from the rough furniture there seemed to be only a couple of shelves which held tin plates, a couple of mugs and a blackened coffee-pot.

There was no fireplace. So she guessed all the cooking was done on a communal fire. Were all the cabins this sparse, she wondered. If so, she pitied the women and the children existing in such primitive conditions.

She was thirsty and her back and legs ached from the unaccustomed riding. She forced herself to sit on the bed, but moved quickly when she felt the first bite from a flea.

She prowled the room like a she-cat as she waited. She both dreaded the big man's coming back and hoped for it. Anything to get out of the fetid atmosphere. The suspense was killing her.

As she explored the room she found a long-handled besom made from hazel twigs bound to a straight larch pole. So someone had tried to keep this muckhole in some kind of order, she thought, as she tested the broom for weight. It might be heavy enough to use as a weapon. . . .

It came to her suddenly. She must stand behind the door when he unbarred it, and hit him before he knew just where she was. With luck, she might stun the man mountain and flee into the stunted bushes before he came round.

Just what she should do after that, she daren't think about, but any kind of freedom was better than what awaited her otherwise.

She hitched up her skirt and petticoats, adjusting her leather belt to take up the extra material. If she had to run, she didn't want to be hampered by a long skirt.

She waited, and waited.

She could hear screams and yells from both men and women outside. It sounded like a drunken orgy. As darkness fell, her courage ebbed. She thought of Billie and consoled herself that he *might* have followed her at a distance. At least that disgustingly filthy man didn't know he was out there.

She was trembling when at last she heard the rattle of the wooden plank being taken off the door. It swung ajar. Silhouetted against the glare of the fire stood the tall broad figure of Barnaby.

The door was thrust open quickly and Sarah had to drag in her breath and her stomach so that the creaky door didn't actually touch her.

She waited. He did not move but stood there adjusting his eyes to the dim interior. He looked around and gave a great bellow. She hadn't bargained for this. She'd thought he'd come straight in and she would have hit him before he realized something was wrong.

'Come out, wherever you are and don't play games with me,' he bawled. He came inside the cabin and bent towards the bed, wrenching off the bearskin. That was when Sarah struck, but the larch pole broke when it came in contact with Barnaby's head. He howled and swore as he fell to his knees but he caught her ankle as she tried to run out of the open door.

She fell but lashed out with her feet, catching his arm, but he was on top of her before she could scramble away.

'You little bitch! You think you can get away from me? I'll show you!' He struggled to get both her wrists in one hand while she squirmed and fought and had the satisfaction of digging her teeth into his chin and drawing blood.

Then, puffing and panting, with sweat running in rivulets down her cheeks, she lay imprisoned, her wrists held tightly. She tried to bring her knee up to his groin, but he'd been in too many fights not to be aware of that move. He slapped her hard on each cheek and her eyes closed as the world seemed to spin around.

He began fumbling at his belt. She heard her bodice rip but it was at a distance. It was as if it was happening to someone else, and the darkness came down.

A figure appeared in the doorway. There was

blood oozing from a shoulder wound. He leaned against the jamb, panting.

'Barnaby, what the hell's going on? We're being surrounded. Can't you hear the gunfire?'

Barnaby jerked away from the still figure under him. Goddammit to hell! He was just in the mood for a bit of young stuff.

'What the hell are you talkin' about, Pete?'

'Jesus! Are you loco or somethin'? I've just rode in and there's no one on guard and there's merry hell goin' on down the mountain! They're comin' up fast!'

'Who are, you stupid bastard?'

'Them bloody Carradines! I told you it was a mistake to rob their traps!'

All thoughts of raping Sarah vanished. Barnaby was on his feet in a flash, buttoning up his pants and slapping his belt around himself.

'Ah, stow it, Pete, you're an old woman! We can take on the lot of them! They're a pissproud bunch at best of times!'

'This time they got help, Barnaby. They got strangers with long-range rifles.'

'How the hell d'you know?'

' 'Cos I had a hard time comin' through, man. I nearly never made it. They saw me and came after me. They was shootin' to kill, Barnaby.'

'Shit!' He looked at the sweating Pete who looked all in.

'Come on, you can still ride?' Pete nodded.

'If you give me a slug of that redeye of yours.'

'Aye, I can do better than that. I can give you a snort of the real stuff,' and he handed over one of Tot Crayshaw's bottles of whiskey.

Pete drank hard and burped and Barnaby dragged the bottle away from him.

'Give over, Pete, or you'll drop in your tracks! Now let's away and see what the boys are doing about these assholes.'

Pete looked at Sarah lying on the ground.

'What you doing about her?'

'Oh, she's goin' nowhere. She'll be safe enough in here. She'll never get out. He laughed and slammed the door behind them both and put the heavy plank into place.

The gunfire could be clearly heard now. The Carradine bunch were sure making a song and dance about losing a few beaver pelts. Maybe it had been a mistake to raid them, especially if the Carradine brothers had reinforcements.

Still, Barnaby took heart. Their settlement was hard to reach. Half a dozen men could hold the only way in to the tiny valley tucked away high up in the hills leading to the higher mountain range.

It was a fortress and they could hold out for ever as long as they had water and grub.

The worry for Barnaby was the news of the long-range rifles, weapons which they did not have. He took heart in thinking of the two extra hunting rifles and the brace of pistols taken from the dead father of the girl. There had been a limited amount of ammunition too. It would all help. He cursed the fact that their own stock of ammunition was getting low.

He cheered up when he remembered that the Carradines themselves were no gunhawks. They concentrated on trapping and grazing a few sheep on the high pastures. They would soon get sick of trying to take out Barnaby Dougan and his men. Others had tried it and none had succeeded.

He did wonder who had joined up with Tucker Carradine and why they had taken potshots at Pete, who was riding in to the camp. It didn't look as if they were on the prod because of the traps. They were looking for a man on the move.

Grabbing his own guns and loading up, he nodded grimly at Pete.

'Let's show the bastards we mean business!'

Billie Devonport crouched in the bushes. He watched the big hairy mountain-man drag Sarah from the wagon. He felt shame. It had been sheer impulse that had sent him tumbling from the wagon: self-preservation. It had only been when he was lying panting and cowering under cover that he realized he'd abandoned her. He should have stayed and fought the big ape

Billie's teeth rattled with fear. He was a farm boy from Ontario, not a wild bar-room brawler, he told himself. What could he have done without a gun?

At twenty, Billie was inexperienced and this was a hell of a way to become a man. Holy mother of God! The old man dead and Sarah . . . what in, hell would they do to her?

He watched the looting of the wagons, the feverish excesses of the savages who took delight in the wanton destruction of Tot Crayshaw's goods that were no good to them. He saw the men pull Tot's clothes from portmanteaux and laugh over them and wave Sarah's intimate garments above their heads in drunken abandon.

He saw the drinking of Tot's store of whiskey and his fear mounted for Sarah.

Then the youth who found Tot's strong-box stopped all that. A shot from a gun, and the box was opened and Billie stared as Tot's savings in loose dollar bills erupted into the air and the breeze carried them away.

He watched while men darted everywhere with greedy outstretched hands to catch the bills that danced and fell like leaves in the Fall.

A great bellow from the big man who was the leader sobered them all up. There was a flurry of sorting and packing of what might be useful to them and then the struggle of loading everything on the eight wagon horses, which were not used to being worked as packhorses. Then the wagons themselves were shunted down the slope to smash into kindling. Tot's body was flung into a crevasse and the cavalcade started to make their way upward into the higher reaches of the mountain.

Billie followed well behind. The trail was easy to follow. The men sang as they went, happy at the outcome of the raid.

Billie shivered. Night was falling and the temperature was dropping. His heavy beaver jacket had been in the wagon and now someone else was wearing it. He was hungry and thirsty too. It was a long time since his last meal.

He could smell coffee and roasting meat on a huge blazing camp-fire in the middle of several lean-to soddys and a couple of wind-bleached shacks.

He'd watched for hours the comings and goings of the trappers clad in their half-cured skin jerkins and ragged breeches. Most wore beaver hats with tails still attached. The big man wore a greasy wide-brimmed Stetson that made him look even bigger and more formidable.

He was surprised to see a handful of sullen women and several small children, all grouped round the camp-fire. The women seemed to work together to produce food.

They'd watched the cavalcade come into camp with dull eyes and avid looks at Sarah. The only show of interest was when the big man tossed Sarah's belongings to them and they fell on them like wolves fighting over a carcass.

He was agonizing over Sarah's imprisonment in one of the shacks and his imagination was getting out of hand because of the silence and the knowledge that the big man was alone inside with her. God! How he wished he'd had a gun!

Then the gunfire came and he pricked up his ears. What in hell was happening? The fusillade of shots came from further down the mountain. Someone out there was moving around in the darkness who shouldn't have been and was now being shot at by the big man's guards.That meant that he too should take care. The guards could be anywhere.

Then a horseman galloped into camp and slid off his mount before it was still. He was running drunkenly to the shack which Billie guessed belonged to the big man.

The newcomer didn't knock but burst inside unceremoniously and a few minutes later both men hurried out, the big man only pausing to shut the plank door and put the plank firmly into place.

There was a hurried discussion with the men around the camp-fire and then Billie watched the men disappear into the brush, guns in hand. They were expecting trouble.

Billie looked at the door of the shack. There was a clear space in front of it. He could rush it, risk being fired on, or he could take his time and climb a hillock behind it and sneak around the walls and trust to luck. Again he wished he had a gun.

He waited and watched for a few minutes. An old man with a gun came into view and threw on a few more logs on to the fire. He seemed to be the only guard left in camp.

Meanwhile the gunfire was intermittent. It was as if someone was playing hide and seek.

Billie saw the old man cock his ear as if listening to the progress of the battle. He made a cigarette and lit it from a twig pushed into the fire. Then he moved over to a tree and urinated and Billie saw his chance.

Running on his toes, he moved with surprising speed. He had the plank off the door and was inside the shack before the man turned around. He stood leaning against the door to get his breath back and then moved sharply as an object came flying through the air at him. He ducked.

'I don't know who you are,' growled Sarah, 'but you won't take me alive!' The next minute she was lunging at him, with arms and legs flailing. She got in a couple of punches and a kick on the shins before he caught and shook her.

'Stop it, Sarah! It's me, Billie! For God's sake, be quiet!'

He felt Sarah sag in his arms.

'It's . . . it's really you?'

'Yes, it's me and I want to get you out of here, so don't you start crying and going all female on me.'

But Sarah cried and Billie slapped her cheeks lightly to shock the fear out of her. She became angry.

'You hit me!'

'Yes, and I'll do it again if you go soft! Listen to me.' He shook her to get all her attention. 'I want you to go out there and talk to that old man. I think he's the only one left in the camp. Flirt with him if you have to.'

'And what are you going to do?'

'I'm going to creep up behind him and clobber him. I want his guns. We must have his guns!'

He felt her nod in the darkness. She took several deep breaths. On impulse he kissed her. He'd never kissed her before. He knew old Tot hoped that they would marry in the future but until now they had only been friends who liked each other. Now he felt an age-old primitive feeling of protecting his woman.

Billie was growing up fast.

Three

Hank Bodell was having second thoughts about throwing in with the Carradine brothers. They were tall gaunt shambling men, all with looks of predatory hawks. His thigh pained him. It was only a flesh wound but it was making riding damned awkward. What had kept him going so far was his anger at having been shot at and losing the best herd of mustangs he'd seen in months, especially the palomino-type stallion. There weren't many throwbacks as good as that one in the mountains.

As he and his three young riders had gone careering after the hidden marksman, the disadvantage of playing hide and seek with a man who evidently knew the terrain had come home to them.

Exhausted, and with Hank tempted to call it a day, they'd met up with the Carradines who were brewing coffee amidst a smelly mound of skins, which the youngest member of the family was baling and loading up on a couple of ancient and bony pack mules.

The youngster, Luke, gawped at them with an idiot's slack mouth before running off and pointing them out to a man crouching around a camp-fire. Strange sounds had issued from the boy's mouth. He looked frightened of strangers.

The older man stood up with a bound and faced them as they rode in, pointing an old-fashioned blunderbuss in their direction.

'Hold it right there, fellers, or I'll blow the head off the one who moves!'

Hank and his men froze, and watched the hawk-faced man walk with a cat's fluid stride towards them. He was wearing deerskin trousers and jacket with fringes running across back and sleeves for the rain to drip from, and heavy long-legged moccasins such as Indians wore. On his head was a badly-cured beaver cap with a broad tail hanging down his back. He smelt from ten yards.

He studied the four men, fanning the blunderbuss gently and Hank held his breath. Those old blunderbusses had a habit of going off and if properly charged could be lethal.

'What you doin' in these parts?' The words came out slowly as if he wasn't used to communicating.

'I'm Hank Bodell and these are Ed, Charlie and Paddy and we're huntin' a man with a long-range rifle? Do you know of one around here?'

There was a click behind Hank. He risked a look and saw two other men who must have been the first man's brothers; because they were so astonishingly alike. His horse danced a little at the disturbance and he cursed under his breath.

The first man glanced at one of the newcomers.

'You know of a man who totes a long-range rifle, Bill?'

'No, Tucker. There be only the old hermit feller who lives alone, unless it be the Dougan clan. Maybe one of them has such a gun.'

'Ah, now that's a thought.' Tucker scratched his bristly chin.

'What you want him for, mister?'

'He took a potshot at me. Brought me down and we lost a herd through him, damn him to hell!'

'So your outfit's one of them scaring the hell out of the mustangs?'

'Not scaring 'em, culling them is a better expression.'

'Hmm, same thing. You've got 'em all of a twitch.'

Hank eyed the coffee-pot.

'Mind if we share your coffee?'

Tucker Carradine considered. 'If you're an enemy of the Dougans you're more than welcome.'

'The Dougans, who're they?'

'They live further up the mountain, God rot 'em! They're mean enough to kill the lot of you! I could bet that bale of skins, Barnaby Dougan is the man you're looking for! Come on down and I'll tell you about him. I expect you could eat some pickled pork too?'

Hank breathed a sigh of relief and glancing at the other three men gave a slight shrug and dismounted. The others followed. They were thirsty. The coffee smelled good and their guts rumbled for grub.

The young lad, Luke, produced surprisingly good bread and a large cut of belly pork from a saddle bag, Tucker sliced great thick wads of pork from the joint and Bill and his brother Jed dished out hunks of fresh bread. All held their broad-bladed Bowie knives as they ate. Hank took it as a hint that if all was not well, they were armed and ready to use their knives.

The young boy, Luke, ate with the clumsiness of a small child.

'What's wrong with him?' Hank asked bluntly.

'Fell on his head when he was a baby,' Tucker said laconically. 'Ma's pet. He's good for doing chores. A good lad is Luke. Wouldn't hurt a fly.'

Hank nodded. 'Now what about these Dougans?'

'I got a proposition for you, mister. They're a dangerous crazy bunch. Call themselves trappers but they're just a bunch of mountain hoodlums, lazy bastards who prey on anyone fool enough to try taking short cuts through the mountains.They've taken women prisoners, keep 'em. Oh, yes,' he saw Hank Bodell's look of surprise, 'there's women up there who've been there for years, have kids. I know, we've seen 'em.'

'Can't you do anything about them?'

Tucker Carradine laughed. 'Why man, there's only us up here and our ma and Tilly our sister. What can we do? There must be twenty or more of them. Besides, they live in a small valley up there with only one way in. It's a bloody fortress, that's what it is.'

Hank looked at him consideringly. 'Then what's your proposition? You're not suggesting we go up there and wipe 'em out? We're not gunhawks, we're bronc-busters.'

'You got it wrong, mister. We don't need to go up there. Some of them sneak out and raid our traps for meat, Barnaby Dougan is one of them. I reckon Barnaby is the feller you want. He's the brains of the bunch. We can pick 'em off like sitting ducks!'

'Why haven't you done it before?'

Tucker Carradine looked uncomfortable and shrugged. 'We've tried it but there's not enough of us . . . now. They killed my pa and my two older brothers and a coupla cousins. Pa was the one who got mad when they raided our traps. A reglar fightin' machine he was. But they shot him and strung him up as a warnin'. Bastards!'

'So you reckon we can do what your pa did?'

'Hell! Four extra men could do a lot of damage and you'd get your man. If Barnaby was strung up . . .'

'In revenge for your pa?'

'Yeh, why not? Tit for tat I say. It's a matter of cutting off the snake's head and the rest will die. They'll all want to get out of that valley. There's young fellers up there who'll want to see a bit more of the world.'

'Don't you?'

'It's different for us. We're free to come and go. We live up here because it's our home. They're not born and bred up here. They're all fugitives, scum left over from the war and wanted men.'

'What about the women and kids?'

Tucker shrugged and then grinned in a wolfish manner. 'We could do with a few women amongst us. We can take 'em in or let 'em go to town. We only have Ma and Tilly. You want a woman? You can have Tilly, she's on heat as soon as she sees a feller, any feller!'

Hank shook his head. 'I don't know about these young bucks but you can count me out. I've got a woman of my own.'

'So you'll come in with us? Not that you have much choice, mister,' and Tucker waggled the old gun. Hank took the hint. He looked round at the silent brothers. All except Luke, who was picking his teeth, were now staring at him, a slight smile on their faces. God! They looked a wild bunch! There was nothing to stop them killing the lot of them and leaving the bodies to the buzzards!

'Yeh, you can count us in,' Hank managed to say casually, hiding any concern he felt in the situation.

But now he was having second thoughts on the whole operation. They'd waited until Tucker reckoned that the Dougans would be on the prod, looking for meat. They'd staked out the traps set on the lower ground where the big stuff wandered, grazing. There were several pits dug and covered over with branches and sods arranged along paths used by deer and antelope. Sometimes there were two beasts down there in the pit, a half-eaten deer and a mountain cat or wolf and because the walls of the pit were sloped with a overhang, the big cats could not escape. A mountain cat was a prize indeed. The pelts fetched good prices back in town. It meant many luxuries in food and bits and bobs for Tilly and Ma. Everyone was pleased when they had a double catch even though half the meat might be eaten.

The skirmish had started early. Hank was amazed at how silently the Carradines could move through the brush. Hank and his men followed more clumsily but stayed still in the places Tucker indicated.

Hank's leg hurt. His thigh throbbed. He wished like hell he'd stayed with Linx and the others, but now there was no going back. He still felt a certain rage against the man who'd downed him and lost him that herd. His rage helped to make him endure the wait.

Tucker had said Barnaby Dougan was a big gorilla of a man, not to be mistaken. Hank would like the satisfaction of shooting him. Then he and the boys could get back to the business of catching broncs.

Suddenly there were the staccato sounds of gunfire further away. Hank tensed. So Tucker was right. They were being raided. Hank cocked his rifle and made sure his Colts were loosened a little in their holsters. He was strung up, a bit nervy. Hell! He was no gunfighter!

Then it happened. A figure was battering his way through the brush at headlong speed. In the deceptive moonlight it looked like a boy. Chre-ist! Hank thought, is he friend or foe? but soon got his answer as Bill Carradine came whooping up behind him, firing as he went. Hank sent off a half-hearted shot. His heart wasn't in it. All he wanted was the big man in his sights.

Suddenly the gunfire grew louder. Screams and yells came as the skirmishing intensified. Ed Gittens, supporting a wounded Charlie Nelson, struggled to where Hank crouched. Hank nearly pulled a trigger on both, but Ed's agonized whisper stayed his hand.

'Hank! For God's sake help me with Charlie. He's got a slug in his shoulder!'

'Lay him down here,' Hank answered tersely. 'Where's Paddy?'

'Out there somewhere with Tucker. That bastard's using us, Hank. I sure wish we'd never come on this lark! There's more of them than that bastard made out!'

'You go after Paddy and get him back here fast. I'll look after Charlie. We're getting out of here.'

Ed sloped off and Hank bound up Charlie's bleeding shoulder with Ed's bandanna. They'd have to probe for the bullet when they got back to camp.

Hank cursed. It was bad enough having a gammy leg himself but to have Charlie out of the game for the next few weeks was frustrating. The outlook for the success of the mustang-catching expedition could be doomed without enough fit men to hunt with.

Paddy O'Rourke came back with Ed Gittens spitting blood from a tooth knocked out in a short but violent fight with a stinking barbarian, which was how Paddy described him.

'To be sure, begorra, they're not men, they're bloody animals and that's the right of it,' he spluttered as he mopped up his mouth and chin. 'If it wasn't for Ed here, I'd be a goner! Stuck him in the back like the pig he was! Good on yer, Ed. I owe you one!'

'We're getting out. Now. Fast, before Carradine knows what's happening. If he wants to fight with those bastards, let him get on with it.'

'What about the big feller? Don't you want to get him?'

'Forget him. I just want to get back to camp.'

'We could have the Carradines on our trail!'

'Look, we're not hanging around. We'll get out of this cursed country and go hunting mustangs. We'll follow the trail of that herd. I want that palomino.'

Ed nodded.

'Just as you say, Hank. You're the boss.'

Billie watched Sarah with some concern. She was flagging. Sweat streamed down her face and her long black hair was wet and hanging like rats' tails.She looked more like a squaw than a white girl. Her clothes were torn and she had trouble keeping herself decent because of her attacker ripping her bodice.

He wanted her badly. God, how he wanted her. Every bit of bare flesh from her ankles to the teasing sight of warm flesh through ripped cloth urged him to take her.

He swallowed. Until now they had been friends. He couldn't possibly do anything to spoil that relationship. Let her down now and if they ever got back to civilization, his chances with her would be gone.

'Sarah? Do you want to rest?'

She turned her white face to his. He saw how haggard she'd become. He was thirsty and hungry and so must she be. They had not come across a stream and the night was coming in cold. To survive they would have to huddle together for warmth.

'No. I want to go on. We must find that trail. It's the only way to get out of these mountains.'

'It's nearly dark, Sarah. We could be walking in circles.'

'Pa said travellers watch the stars when they travel

by night. We'll watch the stars, Billie.'

'I'm hungry, Sarah. Maybe we should stop and I'll try and catch us something to eat.' He held up the rifle he'd taken from the old man in the camp.'

Suddenly Sarah started to cry and Billie took her in his arms.

'Don't cry, Sarah, we'll get out of this, you'll see.'

She sniffed. 'Oh, Billie, what will become of us? Pa's dead and we've got nothing and we're lost and I'm frightened.'

Billie felt his heart swell in his chest. He'd look after her. He didn't know how, but he would. He'd protect her and even die for her if necessary. He sat her down under a tree.

'Look, I'm going to have a look around. You sit still and rest and I'll see what I can find. There must be something to eat around here. If the Indians can survive, so can we.'

'But they know what to look for. We don't!'

Billie closed his eyes and sighed. She was certainly spelling it out for him. He was just an ignorant farm boy and she knew it. He was determined to show her differently.

It was then they heard the gunfire faint but distinct in the distance. Hell! Those bastards must be under attack but by whom? Hope galvanized him into action. Maybe it was a posse from the last town they'd stayed at. Maybe those gorillas were a well-known bunch and it was a surprise raid. There could have been other travellers attacked like they had been. Maybe they would be able to join another group on the way to Wyoming!

He started to run towards the gunfire. He must find out what was going on. Then he paused and looked back at Sarah slumped under the tree. If anything happened to him she would be lost. Helplessly, he knew he couldn't leave her. All he could do was to forage around, maybe catch some nocturnal animal or come across a thicket of hazel-nuts or blueberries. Vaguely he knew that there were nuts and fruits to look out for.

He never saw or heard the old man come up behind him, but felt the hard blow on the back of the neck and then all went black. . . .

Elijah Joe booted the boy over and peered down at Billie, scratching his chin as he did so. This wasn't the idiot boy of the Dougan clan. He must be one of them damned bronc-busters and he deserved all he got, coming into the mountains like hellriders and chasing the mustangs to all hell and back, never considering mares in foal or young 'uns who might not be able to keep up with the herd and be left to die of hunger. For when the leaders got spooked, they stayed spooked and galloped off into new territory.

The bronc-busters would get short shrift with him.

Still, this youth didn't have the look of a long-term bronc-buster. He wasn't dressed like no cowboy he'd come across. For one thing he didn't wear a holster and a hand-gun. He was carrying an old rifle which didn't say much for his marksmanship. He was also dressed in all-in-ones which Elijah Joe described as dungarees. This kid looked more like a dirt farmer than a cowpoke.

He was in two minds to leave him lying there. He didn't want company. He was out doing the rounds of his own traps.He already had a brace of jack rabbits and a hatful of prairie-chicken eggs. He could go home, cook a meal and go to bed and forget this. He could mind his own business.

Then, thinking of the mountain cats which prowled at night and could scent a man from a mile away, he knew that he couldn't leave this kid. A man, yes; he could have left an older man with no bad conscience. But this kid. . . . He yanked him to his feet and slapped his cheeks.

'Come on, kid, open your eyes. Wakey wakey!'

Billie blinked and looked at the old man cross-eyed. His head thumped and he felt sick. He put a cautious finger up to where it hurt. Jesus! The bump was as big as a goose's egg! He wondered what had hit him and then as his brains began to work, realized this tough looking old nut was the one who'd done it.

'What the hell . . . who're you?' he asked as he tenderly rubbed the bump.

'I might say the same about you, son. You're not a Dougan. Are you with those bronc-busters?'

'What bronc-busters?' He peered at Elijah Joe.

'If you're not with that wild bunch, just who are you?'

Elijah Joe spat on the ground.

'I'm Elijah Joe and I live alone. If you're not with those bronc-busters just what are you doing crashing about like a clumsy bull attracting attention from cats to wolves on the prowl? Are you loco or something?'

Billie gulped. He hadn't realized he was being so clumsy. Hell! He had a lot to learn out here in the wild country, that was, if he lived long enough!

'I didn't know I was crashing about as you put it. I was foraging about for some food.'

'Then you wouldn't catch anything the way you were moving around. I was watching you. Think yourself lucky it was me that crept up behind you and not a cat!'

Suddenly, Billie's guts churned. He thought of Sarah, left alone under that tree, an unsuspecting victim for a hungry cat.

Elijah Joe saw the sudden fear on his face.

'What is it, man?'

'I left Sarah . . . alone under a tree . . . I didn't think . . .'

Elijah Joe jumped. 'A woman! You left a woman alone out here in these woods? What are you! Some kind of city dude or something? Come on, let's get back to her.' He gave Billie a shove to get him going. 'Which direction?'

Billie looked around helplessly. 'I . . . I think it

was this way.' He set off along a faint trail that might have been his own tracks.

'You're sure about this? Did you take note of the stars?'

'N . . . no.' I just took off. We were hungry. I was looking for food.'

'Dumbhead! Christ! You're more helpless than a baby! Get those legs movin', feller. We might have to cast around for her.'

They heard distant gunfire as they moved forward. Billie held his breath and concentrated on moving as quietly as the old man. He watched his movements and tried to follow suit, being careful about putting a foot down on dry twigs and easing muscles in his legs so that each stride distributed his weight evenly.

Then they heard a faint scream and a thrashing in the undergrowth as if someone was running headlong. Then a shot that sounded shockingly close and then all was still.

Billie's heart beat violently and the old man cursed.

'What you think's happening?' Billie gasped.

'Someone's copped it by the sound of it,' Elijah Joe muttered. 'I hope it isn't what I think!'

They were coming to a place Billie dimly recognized. He'd passed that great redwood tree when he'd left Sarah. There had been a clearing of sorts and now he ran ahead to where Sarah should be.

She wasn't there.

Stupidly he looked around him.

'Sarah? It's me, Billie. If you're hiding, you can come out now.'

He peered into the trees and mass of undergrowth, expecting to see her emerge. She was hiding. His mind wouldn't entertain any other explanation.

He stood waiting. Helpless. Inexperienced. A farm boy again with no knowledge other than that of farming a small homestead with a boss who told him what to do.

A tap on the shoulder made him start.

'She ran thataway.' Elijah Joe pointed with his thumb into the blackness of the trees. 'Come on, we must follow her tracks.'

They found her sprawled under a bush. There was blood seeping from a shoulder wound. She wasn't dead. They could see her fingers still clawing at the ground. The scream they'd heard was from her as she'd been gunned down like an animal.

Billie stared down at her in disbelief. He began to shake as he watched Elijah Joe bend down and examine her wound. He stood upright, his old bones creaking. He grinned at Billie.

'She'll live. Got a nasty flesh wound and it won't look so pretty when it's healed, but she'll live. Come on, young feller, you're younger than me. Lift her up and we'll take her back to my place and then you can tell me why the pair of you are acting like babes in the wood! I'm mighty curious.'

*

Hank Bodell looked down at the girl he'd shot. Chre-ist! It must be that Tilly, sister of the Carradines! Now there would be hell to pay! The Carradines would be after their blood when they found her!

He looked at Ed and Paddy who were looking nervously down at the girl.

'Is she dead?' asked Ed.

'Christ! I don't know. She ain't movin'.'

'What'll we do with her? We can't leave her.'

'Yes, we can. She looks dead anyway.'

'But . . .' Hank glanced at Paddy who was turning away in a kind of disgust.

'Look, Ed, we heard her running. We all thought it was one of them Dougans. We were wrong but we didn't know that. I'm sorry I hit her, but we've got to be realistic. We've got Charlie to get back to camp. We can't be bogged down with someone else! It don't matter what we said, it wouldn't go down well with those wild bastards up there! They'll string us up! So let's just forget it happened and scarper! We'll go get the horses and get back to camp.'

Linx Firman, along with Ned and Abe, reined in his horse and looked out over the distant valley surrounded by dark purple-blue mountains. It was an ideal place to be at dawn when the sun's rays were just coming up over the far horizon, and painting everything in pink and golden hues. The trees, still shadowed in parts, showed up clear and bright, a clean sharpness in the air which smelled of pine, sage and an undefinable mix of herbage, grass and rain to come.

Linx sighed. These mountains would be a great place to settle down. His keen eye saw movement and guessed that a herd of mustangs was just over the far hills. Yes, a ranch up here in the hills, away from danger and predators would be an ideal life. Especially if there was no lone marksman out there to spoil the peace.

He was looking for signs of Hank and his boys. He raised his glasses to his eyes and peered into the increasing light. The trees and terrain were thrown into sharp focus. He could even see a narrow meandering stream moving leisurely down on the valley floor. A great place for grazing horses. He must tell Hank about that when they met up. A good place to wait for horses coming to drink.

He shook his head.

'No sign of them, fellers. We'll have to ride on a piece and watch and wait. Good grazing down there. We might catch that palomino and his mares down there after all.'

Abe grinned. 'Maybe we should forget the boss and take a look-see. If he wants to go gallivantin', it doesn't mean we should!'

Ned laughed and agreed with him. 'Yeh, we're not paid to hunt varmints who take potshots at

Hank! It's his business if he wants to waste valuable hoss-catchin' time.'

Linx nodded.

'You gotta point. Maybe we should explore the country and see what's on offer. I sure thought I saw a herd over that far ridge. Maybe you're right. We should take a look-see.'

They rode on down into the valley, pausing to drink and water their horses by the small stream. The water was crystal clear and cold, a sure sign that its source was far up past the snowline well into the mountains.

Linx dowsed his sweating head and swatted mosquitoes attracted by his sweat.

'This sure is God's own country,' he remarked, looking around appreciatively. 'Plenty of timber for a cabin that would withstand cold winters, not too far from civilization for stocking up on grub and yes, look up there, a herd of deer, by God! What more could a man want?'

'A good woman who could cook and a bad 'un to go to bed with!' Abe joked.

Linx cocked a knowing eye at Abe.

'I thought you was past all that, bub! You was saying only the other day you'd forgotten what it was all about!'

'Yeh, well, I still got ideas in m'head. A feller can dream, can't he?'

Ned laughed. 'So that's what you get up to when you shout out in yor sleep? I thought you sure had stones in yor bunk mattress, like, I'll tell old Cookie not to get you a new one when we get back to the ranch! He was for gettin' you one!'

'Gerraway with you!' and Abe flicked water at Ned. 'I bet you wouldn't know what to do with a bad woman!'

'Just hand me a bad woman and I'll show you!'

'You always were a piss-proud sonofabitch, Ned!' He winked at Linx who was grinning at both of them as he felt around in his saddle-bags for the coffee makings and some of Jake's panbread and a hunk of pickled pork.

'Stop ribbin' each other and rustle up some firewood and let's us have a fire goin'.' Linx diverted their minds to grub because the banter might have escalated into a more serious argument. It had happened before and it could happen again. It was always dangerous to talk about women, especially for men who hadn't seen a woman in months.

The coffee-pot was soon emitting a stomach-churning aroma under a skilfully piled mound of dead wood positioned over a round of flat stones. The wood being dry gave off little smoke. It was the green stuff that gave off the thick black smoke which the Indians used to blanket their messages. Now, they needed to be discreet. No need to let anyone watching and wondering know their location.

When hungry stomachs had been appeased with thick slabs of pork and Jake's panbread washed down with thick strong black coffee, all three felt drowsy with food, the heat of the fire and the peaceful quality of their surroundings.

Linx hunkered lower, his back against a tree. He shoved his hat over his eyes and gave a groan.

'This sure beats chasin' after hosses.'

'Yeh,' Abe agreed. 'It gives us time to let the blisters heal on our arses!'

He too wriggled and made himself comfortable.

'Hey, Ned, your turn to keep watch!'

'What's there to watch?' Ned asked dozily.

'Just a thought,' Abe answered. 'Maybe one of us should.'

'Shurrup!' Linx said sleepily. 'You're frightening the birds!'

Then suddenly he was sitting up, wide awake, his spine tingling as it did when something was wrong. He looked about him. What in hell was it? Then he realized. The birds! They were flapping their wings and cawing and making a to-do about taking off into the sky to fly in agitated circles above their roosting places. Linx sprang to his feet, hand on gun, looking about him.

'On your feet, fellers. We got company!' Suddenly he was staring into the muzzles of three six-guns firmly held by three of the wildest-looking men he'd ever seen.

They smelled of buffalo fat from twenty paces. They were tall, gaunt, with sharp pointed features like animals. All had shaggy hair and were dressed in skins and rags. They looked like brothers. Linx caught his breath. Mountain men. Linx had heard of the savage mountain men and been warned to look out for them.

'Howdy, fellers,' Linx began and stopped when all three guns were cocked as the three men glided forward in a peculiar catlike movement. He froze as did Abe and Ned. None of them was prepared to gamble his life on heroics.

'Hands up real slow,' the oldest and their leader said. 'Bill, look snappy and collect their guns while they introduce theirselves. Now, mister,' looking at Linx, 'what you be doin' in these here parts?' He lifted his gun menacingly.

Linx's hands went up as he watched the gun, his heart going like a trip-hammer. He wondered whether these sons of bitches were cannibals too.

'I'm Linx Firman and these are Abe and Ned. Might I ask who you are?'

'It don't matter who we are. What we want to know is whether you be with those other strangers who come into our country and stir up our wild life?'

Linx was conscious of a great unease. What had happened to Hank and the boys? Had these wild creatures killed them?

'Some of our men are missing. We're out here to catch mustangs, but someone took a pot-shot at our boss. He and some of the boys went hunting him.'

'Aye, that would be Barnaby Dougan. He and his brothers live in a goddamn fortress of a place high up in the mountains.' He spat on the ground and grinned, showing gaps in his yellow teeth. 'That boss of yours would never get him.'

'What happened to Hank and the boys?'

'Who knows? We was on the prod. Those sons of bitches up there have been raidin' our traps and we were out to get 'em. Your boss was persuaded to join us. The fightin' got a bit tough and your boss sure was no real fightin' man. He and the other yeller-livered bastards hightailed it.' He spat in contempt. 'We could have had those Dougans if they'd stayed to fight, and we could have had their women too,' he ruminated softly. 'We could do with some women.'

'So you don't know where they are now?'

'Nope! But we reckon that if we take you back to our place, they'll come lookin' for you.'

'And why would you want them back?'

The older man looked at his two younger brothers and laughed. 'They don't cotton on easy, do they?' The other men laughed with him.

'What don't we cotton on to?' Linx asked evenly.

'Why, if we hold you long enough, they'll come lookin' and they can have you back if they catch us some mustangs. Let's say four mustangs each and one of 'em has to be a stallion, so we can breed our own.'

'Haven't you any hosses?'

'Nope! The last one died two, three years ago. Got mauled by a mountain cat. We ain't had money to buy others and them Dougans always get first pick of any strangers crossing these here mountains. We watched the sons of bitches hold up a coupla wagons a few days ago. Killed an old feller and took off with his daughter. That's how they get their women, the lucky bastards!'

'Didn't you try to help them?'

'Naw, why should we? They was strangers to us. Now if you'll just get your stuff together we'll be on our way. Those are mighty fine ridin' horses you have there and we could do with your coffee-pot and any pans you might have. Ma and Tilly will sure be pleased. Womenfolk like things nice.'

Slowly and reluctantly the three men packed up. There was no chance to turn the tables. Each man worked with a gun pointed at the back of his neck. Linx cursed inwardly.

Then came the long trek back to the Carradine camp. Tucker Carradine kept up a running commentary about all the Dougans' misdeeds and what cut-throats he'd gathered about him. It was a regular town up there in that hidden valley.

'Is there more than one way in?' Linx asked for something to say. Tucker Carradine put a finger to his nose and gave a sly laugh.

'They think there's only one way in, but we know different, don't we, boys?' The brothers gave an amused grin.

'We know this country through and through,' Tucker boasted. 'The trouble with us, there's not enough of us to wipe 'em out. There's only us against twenty or thirty of them. We'll have to take 'em one by one. We must have hit 'em hard last night.'

Again he was brooding about Hank's withdrawal. It was something he hadn't expected.

'We missed a good chance last night. It could be days before they come down to our traps again. You could help us.' He looked consideringly at Linx, 'unless you've got a yeller liver too?'

Linx was angry. 'Look, we come to catch mustangs, not fight other folk's fights! It's none of our business what feudin' goes on. We just want to get on doing what we came out to do, that's all.'

'But what you do is our business, mister! Those mustangs run in our territory!'

'Mustangs you can't catch!' Linx taunted.

'Yeh, well, it's not for want of tryin'. But we reckon you owe us.'

'Yeah?'

'Your boss welched on us. We could have killed 'em, no sweat, but we let them live and they left us in the lurch. That's gratitude for you, and now you're goin' to pay!'

'I think you're mad!'

Tucker Carradine's eyes glittered with a ferocious light.

'The last feller who said that, I blew to Kingdom Come and we buried him with a prayer after drinking up his store of whiskey!'

Linx remained silent. These assholes must be all mad. He gave Abe and Ned a warning glance to take care.

Suddenly the track they were following turned into a gully and on either side were tall cliffs. It looked very much like a dry waddy. The light dimmed as the overhanging cliffs cast a deep shadow. It was like walking through a tunnel, then, just as Linx thought they were going into total blackness, he saw light again at the further end.

Then he was blinking again in the strong sunlight and he saw the gully, opened into a huge crater surrounded by the foothills of distant mountains.

A small log cabin, with a one-man privy some yards from it, stood midst a brown patch of coarse grass. Smoke was rising lazily from a tin chimney and as they moved forward with all three brothers holding guns suggestively, an old woman, presumably Ma, and a young girl came out to watch their approach.

The old woman shaded her eyes to see more clearly. The girl stuck out her chest and started to move towards the newcomers with a smile on her rather pretty face.

'Tilly! Get you back and hold yor hosses!' her mother said sharply. The girl pulled down her lips sulkily.

Linx looked at the two women and the contrast was ludicrous. The old woman was tall and gaunt with the thin hawkish features of her sons, topped off by grey hair drawn back tight into a bun. She wore a man's hunting shirt of deerskin above a ragged black skirt well patched. Her daughter on the other hand was shorter and plumper with heavy breasts that she couldn't hide beneath a man's checked shirt. Her black hair hung untidily to her waist, uncombed and dirty, her rather pretty face grimy and sulky-looking because of her mother's sharp words. There was a smouldering sexiness about her and as she put her hands akimbo she waggled her hips, which were accentuated by the divided skirt she wore.

Her lips puckered and she smiled at Linx when she saw him watching her, her tongue slipping suggestively between thick juicy lips.

Hell, he thought to himself, this girl was ready to explode!

Tucker Carradine saw the look pass between them and grinned.

'What did I tell yer, man? Tilly's a reglar bitch on heat. She killed the last man we caught sniffin' around. She shagged him to death!'

'Tucker!' Ma Carradine's disapproving roar shattered the air. 'It wasn't like that! The preacher had a heart attack! Tilly did her, best for him. . . .'

'Yeh . . . yeh . . . yeh. . . we know, Ma. You've told us often enough but I still say, Tilly shagged him . . .'

'Shut up, Tucker! Go and wash your mouth out! You are always on about Tilly and I won't have it in front of strangers. Who are they?'

Tucker looked sulky while Ma Carradine stepped forward and looked Linx and his men up and down. Tilly was more blatant as hands on hips she encircled all of them in turn and winked at them, leaving all of them with uncomfortably tight pants. She jiggled her magnificent breasts and grinned delightedly as they gulped and tried to look away.

Linx bit his lip. Little bitch! If he got the chance he'd show her what a real man could do! It would take a hell of a long time to shag him to death! He was no goddam preacher!

'Now Ma, don't take on. These here broncbusters are goin' to catch us some mustangs. Then we can ride into town instead of walk and you and Tilly can use the old buggy again. How's that?'

The old woman nodded grudgingly.

'If that's the case, then you'd better come inside and eat. You'll want full stomachs for that.

FOUR

Billie laid Sarah down on what Elijah Joe reckoned was his bed. It was a pile of bracken overlaid with a smelly bearskin. Blood stained her torn bodice, and with shaking hands Billie pulled away the material and exposed the shoulder wound. The sight of it made him feel sick. He felt faint.

Elijah Joe took one look at him and pushed him aside.

'Here, let me tend to it. Rake up the embers of the fire and put on some of them there dried sticks and fill that kettle and boil some water. There's water in that there bucket. Look sharp, son. The longer the bullet's left inside her, the more likely there'll be lead poisonin'. So jump to it, son!'

Elijah Joe didn't wait for Billie's reactions. He got on with the delicate job of swabbing off drying blood around the edges of the wound and assessing the damage. As he did so, he wondered why the

Dougans should shoot at a defenceless girl and why the two young people were in these mountains in the first place.

Trapper, the wolf, lay in a corner on his haunches, watching suspiciously as Billie moved about the small room, his hackles risen and his teeth bared. Billie watched apprehensively and fear made him clumsy.

'You sure that beast won't pounce?'

'Dead sure,' Elijah Joe answered laconically while his old fingers moved fast. 'Mind you, one word from me and all hell will break loose,' and he turned and grinned at Billie, showing dirty yellowing teeth. Billie thought he looked as fierce as his wolf.

Then he was lugging boiling water in an old tin bath across to where Elijah Joe bent over the makeshift bed, the young wolf growling at his heels.

'There you are. How is she?'

'Still out. Now if you get a wad of that there lichen out of that leather bag over there, we'll be ready to dig out the bullet.'

Billie blanched. 'We?'

'Yeh. We.' Elijah Joe glanced up at Billie. 'Haven't you ever helped to dig out a bullet?'

Billie swallowed. 'No. Where I come from we're a peaceable mind-your-own-business kind of folk.'

'Then you haven't lived, son. Now get that wadding while I plunge this here knife into the water and then you'll take hold of her shoulders nice and firm and when she struggles, you hold her down while I dig. Got it?'

Billie nodded dumbly. He couldn't have spoken to save his life. Blindly seeking the lichen, he placed it ready to clap on to the wound when the blood spurted. . . .

He placed his hands on Sarah's shoulders and felt her quiver beneath them. A faint moan issued from her lips.

'Now! Press down hard!' Elijah Joe was digging firmly into the soft flesh of Sarah's shoulder. She began to scream and squirm and Billie grimly held on to her as the old man probed for the bullet. Then suddenly, it popped out, a small cylindrical object glistening a dull bloody silver in the dim light. Billie let out a deep breath of relief as Sarah sagged beneath his fingers in a deep faint.

Elijah Joe held up the slug in triumph.

'There you are, the little bastard! It could have killed her in twenty-four hours! Maybe she'll want to keep it as a memento!'

Billie smiled sickly as he staunched the open wound with the lichen. He knew the importance of lichen. He had used it on farm animals in the past. It helped to clot blood. Now he knew it would help to save Sarah from bleeding to death.

He watched as Elijah Joe bound the lichen to Sarah's shoulder with strips torn off her petticoat. When it was all done to his satisfaction, Elijah Joe produced an earthenware jar of home-brewed pulque. He watered some down in an old tin mug and gave it to her to drink.

It dribbled, but eventually she drank and the shock of it brought her round. She looked about her, seeing Billie.

'Where am I? What's happened?'

'You were shot. This is Elijah Joe and we're here in his soddy. You're safe, Sarah.'

'My . . . my shoulder hurts!' She put up a hand and felt the bulky bandage.

'We had to dig out a bullet, Sarah but you're going to be all right.'

Elijah Joe peered down at her, as Trapper came and sniffed her. She drew back, frightened.

'It's all right, Sarah,' Billie soothed.

Elijah Joe held up the bullet. 'See what I dug out of you! It's your bullet. Take it!'

Sarah held out a hand unbelievingly and took it. It felt strange to be holding something that had caused her so much pain.

She smiled up at Elijah Joe. 'Thank you very much. You are a very kind man.'

Elijah Joe felt a kind of stirring in him. It was as if his hate-filled frozen heart had suddenly started to melt. . . .

'You're welcome,' he said humbly and took himself and his wolf outside to sit in his favourite place, to watch over the familiar panorama of the mountain range and consider these strange new feelings that were now wracking his body.

Trapper sat whining at his feet. He scratched the wolf's head and felt the beast lick his hand.

'All right, boy. We both have a lot to think about. You just behave yourself with them there strangers. They'll soon be gone.' Again he was bewildered and perplexed at the feeling of loneliness that overcame him at his words.

Linx wakened with a start. He and his men were curled up on the floor of a storehouse that smelled of coal oil, coffee beans and rancid bacon. Tucker Carradine had herded them in after they'd been grudgingly fed by Ma Carradine and a simpering Tilly.

Now, Linx looked up to see Tilly bending over him, a key in one hand and Tucker's old gun in the other.

'Wha . . . what d'you want?' Linx asked in a sleepy daze, his wits slow in working.

'What d'you think, big feller? You be nice to me and I'll see you're treated good.' She cast an exploring hand across his chest and down towards his crotch, the key lying where it dropped.

'Hey now, wait a minute!' and Linx drew back in alarm. It was one thing fantasizing what he could do for her, but now, lying beside his men, was a different matter.

'Come on, don't be shy. I thought all you men could do it anywhere.' Tilly launched herself on him like a tigress on her prey, tearing and rending at his shirt and belt.

Abe and Ned heard the scuffling as Linx and Tilly thrashed around the floor. The very attack had put all stirring thoughts out of Linx's head. All he wanted was to get rid of the writhing female who wasn't careful about what she squeezed and pummelled.

'For Christ's sake,' he bawled, 'get the bitch off me!'

Abe, who was nearest, managed to secure a thrashing ankle and gave Tilly's backside a hard tooth-jarring swipe.

That calmed her down a mite, but she glared at Abe, panting and showing her teeth like a vixen.

'What you do that for?' she raved. 'You would have got your turn, him an' all!' She glanced at Ned, who was watching bug-eyed.

Then Tilly, hair all mussed up like rats' tails, loosened her top buttons and showed them her big melons.

'Look what I got, fellers. One of you yeller-livered rats must want to feel 'em!'

Abe and Ned were paralysed. It had been years since the hoary oldsters had been rampant young studs. Linx was not much better but he liked to pay for what he got, for then he was in control. Never in his life had he met a woman like Tilly. He felt as if he'd nearly been raped.

Abe saw the key on the ground and grabbed for it. Tilly saw the move and kicked it under a pile of skins.

'You cain't get away,' she taunted, 'and if you don't play ball with me, I'll see you're fed on scraps, by God, I will!' She lifted up Tucker's gun. 'Who's gonna be first?'

Suddenly there was a ruckus outside the door. The rough planks rattled as Ma Carradine yelled at her daughter.

'Tilly, you little bitch, open up! I know what you're up to, sneaking off from your bed! Just you open this door like a good girl and I'll make you a rag doll. How about that?'

Tilly slowly faced the door.

'I want a real baby, Ma. A doll's no good.'

'Oh, come on, Tilly, open the door and we'll talk about it.'

Tilly laughed and there was a hint of madness in the sound which made Linx's blood run cold.

'We'll talk when I've finished in here and not until! There's three of 'em, Ma. It might be years before I see another man!'

'They're old men, Tilly. You want to wait for a nice healthy young one. Look, next time Tucker goes down to town you and me will go too. Those men are here to catch us horses, Tilly. When we get horses you can go into town as much as you like.'

'And do as I like?' Tilly asked hopefully.

There was a long pause and then Ma Carradine said reluctantly, 'Yes Tilly, you can do as you like.'

Tilly beamed at the men. 'You heard her. She says I'm free to do as I like. What about that then?'

Linx nodded slowly and gave a twisted smile. He was sorry for the girl. Hell! She had a child's mind in a rampant body. He was still wary of her.

'Very nice,' he said lamely.

'Then you'll catch us some horses, mister?'

'Of course, that's what we're here for.'

'Goody good. Then the sooner you start, the sooner we can go into town.'

Just then came another rattling at the door. This time it was Tucker.

'Tilly!' he roared, 'get your arse outa there. This is no time to shag those bastards to death! I want 'em fit enough to catch us some mustangs. Now open this door at once!'

Linx and the boys watched in mute surprise as Tilly meekly hunted for the key and opened the door.

She cowered back as Tucker glared at her, his hand held up to strike her.

'Tucker!' the old woman yelled. Leave her be! I'll watch her.' His hand dropped to his side and he motioned to the girl with his head.

'Go with Ma, Tilly and make us some breakfast. We're off to catch us some mustangs.'

Hank Bodell was in a cold full-blooded rage as he stared at Jake, all alone in the camp.

'The fools! They should have been out there huntin' up mustangs, not going off half-cocked!'

Jake stared at him unimpressed.

'You did, boss. You were hare-brained to go off as you did, and see what you got for your pains. You and Charlie shot and nothing to show for it!'

Jake knew how important he was in this outfit. He cooked well and he doctored the many injuries the men sustained in the tough job of chasing and corralling wild horses. They could be a menace if the stallion leading the herd was young and feisty. Many a man had suffered a broken leg or dislocated shoulder by crowding mustangs and if a man's own horse side-flopped he could be killed instantly. Then there was the danger of having a foot caught in the stirrup and a man being dragged along the ground during a chase. There were many hazards and Jake could cite many cases.

Now he cleaned up Charlie's wound. Fortunately the bullet had gone through Charlie's shoulder from front to back before exiting and it was a case of cleaning and binding up. The loss of blood had already cleaned the wound.

Stoically he listened while Hank raved. Then, turning unceremoniously to him he growled softly, 'Drop yor pants, boss and let me look at that there leg.'

'No need, Jake. Ed bandaged it right good. It don't hurt, just throbs a little.'

'Throbbin' means infection, boss. I'll just take a look.'

Reluctantly Hank dropped his pants and Jake unwound the dirty bandage, exposing a thigh that was swollen and red around the edges of the wound. Jake snorted.

'Not hurtin'? You're a danged fool, boss. I'm gonna have to cauterize it!'

Hank groaned. 'D'you have to? I could do without that.'

'Iffen you want to wait until I have to cut the dangblamed leg off, you'd better let me singe it!'

Hank gritted his teeth.

'Then get to it, but give me the whiskey bottle first!'

He took a long drag from the bottle as Jake sterilized his butcher's knife in the flames of the fire. Then, holding the knife up showing a glowing red, Jake waited until it had cooled some and then cocked an eye to Paddy and Ed.

'Take his shoulders and ankles and hold him down. I don't want him thrashing about.' Then, without more ado, the butcher's knife did the business and the stench of searing flesh assailed them all. Hank fainted but Jake was pleased. He'd saved Hank's leg.

FIVE

Linx Firman walked beside Tucker Carradine, leading his horse and very much aware of the two Carradine brothers close-herding old Abe and Ned. As he walked, he considered their situation: never before had he gone on a mustang hunt with trigger-happy untamed backwoodsmen such as these and especially men who hadn't a horse between them. It was ridiculous! They had no idea of the skill required.

His fear was that disappointment would turn them into killers. He couldn't see how he and his men plus three men, on foot, could chase a herd, direct it into a draw and secure them fast. It took all the cunning of a skilled crew to do just that.

Suddenly he remembered what his old mother had said the day he'd announced he was leaving. Her caustic remark had always stayed with him. 'Linxlater, always steer clear of bad men and loose women and the best of luck to you!'

He snorted at the memory. She'd lived all her life on a remote dirt farm and never realized that the world was full of bad men and loose women.

'Thinking of making a break, mister? I wouldn't try it if I were you. One move and you get it in the back!' Tucker smiled and waggled his gun. Linx gulped. He was no hero.

'Look, if you want mustangs, we gotta range the country. You know these parts better than us. Where's the drinkin' holes that the herds use?'

Tucker pointed into the far distance. Linx could see a haze of foothills with stands of pine and tall grass. It looked good.

'Down by the river over thataway. There's good grass and shelter too. We see 'em sometimes driftin' along. Mebbe we should take a look.'

'Not all of us, we won't. We gotta get windward of 'em and one of us should scout around.'

'Then you go and no funny business or we'll shoot your boys, make no mistake about that!'

Linx looked at Abe and Ned. Hell! If it had been Paddy and Ed he might have made a play, but these oldsters would be too slow. They nodded to him and Ned spat on to the ground.

'You go ahead, boss and we'll wait for yor signal as usual and while you're gone Abe and me will explain the procedure about huntin' the herd into a draw.' Linx nodded, mounted and spurring his horse into a gallop he left the small bunch behind.

As he rode he wondered what had become of

Hank and the boys. It would be a doddle if he could come up with them. They'd show these half-mad assholes a thing or two. . . .

But suddenly his attention was taken by the faint sniff of horses on the breeze. It was that unmistakable smell of a number of sweating animals in a bunch. Quietly he stopped, hobbled his own horse and climbed up a small escarpment. He looked down into a shallow valley; there in the bottom was a narrow winding stream and far down on the valley floor was the sight all bronc-busters valued more than any other: a heaving mass of many-coloured mustangs mingling, some feeding and others drinking at the water's edge.

He saw many fights between stallions as they tried to protect their own females from over-confident stallions wanting to take over.

It was a sight not often seen by white men.

'My my . . .' he whispered to himself as he watched the milling throng, 'if only Hank was here to see this!' He watched in wonder and amazement and tried to count them but it was no good. He reckoned there must be nigh on three hundred animals counting foals and yearlings.

He scrambled back carefully, making sure no watchful animal saw the movement on the skyline. Then he leapt astride his mount and rode back to the others. This would need some careful planning, or else the whole herd would stampede and they would lose the lot.

Abe's and Ned's eyes gleamed when he told of what he had seen. Tucker nodded.

'Yes, we've seen 'em collect together. It's their way of allowin' the young stallions to break away from their mother herds and if they can attract young mares of their own they set up a new remuda. We've seen 'em but we've never had the means to catch 'em ourselves.'

Linx frowned. 'They'll be hard to catch. They'll be more than wild, they'll be vicious when they're all out to catch mares.'

Abe spat again. 'Then we wait until a small herd leaves the rest and go after it. Simple.'

Linx looked at Abe. Simple, eh? It was never simple. What was Abe getting at? Then looking at Tucker, he said softly, 'We might as well save our arses, Tucker.' He dismounted, hobbling his horse so that it could feed. The others followed suit.

Tucker didn't like it. He wanted to rush in and lasso what he could and to hell with the rest.

'You sonofabitch, you're up to somethin'!'

'Nope! Use your head, Tucker. It takes guile to catch hosses! We'll get you hosses when the time's right.'

And with that Tucker had to be satisfied. He sat in brooding silence, cleaning his dirty fingernails with his broad Bowie knife.

Linx watched the sun going down and knew that the mustangs would now come out from the shade trees and eat once again. Their bellies would be full and their speed would be hindered. Now was the time to watch for herds separating and moving on. He got up and stretched.

'Time, boys. If we're goin' to make a round-up now's the time to start.'

Tucker looked eager but puzzled.

'What shall we do?'

'Go take a look yonder and see what they're up to and while we're at it, figure on the nearest draw. We've got to cut the herd out, make it run and guide 'em where we want 'em and that's up a draw which is boxed in. Know of such a place?'

Tucker nodded.

'Dry Bones Creek. Good grass but no water.'

'Good. Then we make for there and while we're roundin' up the herd and doin' the runnin', you boys will be preparin' a brushwood fence. As soon as the last hoss gallops through you swing that fence closed. Understand?'

'Yes, but can you three control them hosses?'

Linx shrugged. 'We can but try. A flanker on each side and one riding drag. That's all we can do. Now if we had Hank and the other boys, we'd have a better chance. But if you do your bit we will do ours. We must at least catch a few stragglers.'

Tucker looked doubtful. It was becoming evident that it wasn't easy, this catching of mustangs.

He climbed the escarpment and watched the herds now beginning to separate and came bounding back down full of excitement.

'They're makin' a move. They're doin' what you said. They're splittin' up!'

'Good. Now let's get ridin'.'

Tucker drew his gun.

'We're not walkin' anywhere, mister while you ride. We're doublin' up with you, until we come on down into the valley.'

Linx shrugged. 'Please yourself, mister. But the horses will sure tire carrying a double load.'

'That's your problem, mister.'

Linx allowed Tucker to leap up behind him. He moved off, conscious of Tucker's gun prodding his spine.

He fervently hoped they wouldn't come across Hank and the others while he was in this position. He didn't fancy getting his spine shattered.

Linx sighed with relief when finally Tucker and his brothers dismounted and got lost in the bushes after pointing out the direction of the draw. Now they could move ahead and surround a herd of mustangs and move them along slowly towards the draw. If it was done right, the animals would not panic and take a headlong run.

It was only when the chief stallion caught on to danger that the situation hotted up. The old stallion tossed his head back and trumpeted; the mares and yearlings milling around him twitched ears, some kicked up heels and a sense of panic swept through the entire mass of animals.

Linx cursed. Had those fools disobeyed his

orders and crept too close? Even an inexperienced yearling would smell those sons of bitches at twenty paces.

The great herd started to disintegrate, a scattering of animals following their own leaders. Linx's mouth watered. If only Hank and the boys had been with them! They could have picked and chosen the best of the bunch!

His eye caught sight of two herds mingling and riding together; one of the leaders was the beautiful palomino. Linx caught his breath. God! What a sight he was, head coming up in defiance, chivvying his mares and nipping at a dappled grey stallion who was fighting to take over his little band. He nodded to Ned and Abe.

'See the palomino! We follow the herd. Ned, you get around to the right and Abe you ride drag and I'll take the left flank. Right?'

Ned and Abe waved their hats. They knew the drill, and Linx pushed forward to ride with the small herd, guiding and turning as he did so.

The fleeing horses saw the strange galloping man-animal, whooping and waving his Stetson and they veered, following their own leader in a blind urge to get away. Foals and yearlings stumbled along behind, chivvied on by Abe who was chasing the stragglers.

This was the time Linx loved best. With the wind in his face, the thunder of many hooves in his ears and the knowledge that his trusty horse could keep up the chase, Linx had time to watch and admire the fluid movement of the wildly galloping beasts. His trained eye picked out those who stood out and would make good riding animals. Some moved more smoothly than others. He saw several likely mares, already concerned and watching out for their foals getting left behind.

A mare concerned for her young would be a good milker and would foal easily. Jesus! They could make a fortune with this lot, if only they'd had Hank and the the boys to help.

Then suddenly the herd broke away and Linx cursed, yelling, and in the excitement of losing them he drew his gun and fired, sending the curving mass of horses into further panic.

Linx knew by Tucker's directions that the herd were in danger of missing the draw. It was as if the old stallion leading the bunch knew that it would be a trap.

The sly old sonofabitch knew! He'd been up that draw before and knew there was no way through.

Linx fired again in a vain attempt to turn the critters and felt a sense of failure. Now what would the Carradine boys do?

Sarah Crayshaw tended the fire. It was cold high up in the mountains and she shivered, pulling the dirty blanket that Elijah Joe had given her further around her. Her shoulder was still stiff and sore and she could only use one hand to do light chores.

Sarah reckoned she'd never met such a peculiar man before. At first she had been frightened of him, then she came to realize that he was frightened of her.

He didn't know much about women and as he never talked much anyway, there was no way to know what he was really thinking.

But he was grudgingly kind. He hadn't much but he'd offered them succour and shelter and he shared his food with them.

Gradually he had opened up to Billie and now they were away on a hunting trip. Elijah Joe had left Trapper at home with Sarah. She had now made friends with the young wolf but was still a little in awe of him. Now he lay at her feet as if he too took comfort from the fire.

'I wonder how long they'll be?' The wolf looked up at her as if he too wondered.

Elijah Joe was giving Billie a lesson in woodcraft. Billie carried one of the old man's ancient shotguns. It felt heavy and awkward and Billie wasn't sure whether he could ever force himself to use it. He was a farm boy not a hunter.

'Now lookit here,' Elijah Joe was saying severely, 'you don't go trampin' through the undergrowth like a wounded buffalo, you go quiet-like.'

'I am! I am, Elijah Joe! Dammit, I can't be much quieter!' Billie protested.

Elijah Joe shook his head in despair. 'Are ye deaf or daffy, lad? A mountain cat or an Injun would hear you comin' at a thousand yards! It's in the vibrations of the ground, lad. You gotta walk as if you're walkin' on air!'

'How?' Billie looked puzzled. Elijah Joe looked puzzled too.

'I dunno.' Elijah Joe scratched his head. 'I was born walkin' light, I guess. You puts yor feet down mighty careful, usin' the muscles of yor legs to balance. You move smooth, like a cat. Go on, try it. You gotta move that way out here in the wilderness. Your life depends on it!'

Billie stepped out carefully, a little stiff-legged and very conscious of each movement. As he did so, a bird flew up from nearly under his feet. It startled him and Elijah Joe gave a grin.

'You be seein' all manner of live things if you be quiet and pass through like a creature of the forest. See, there goes a green snake and over there is the burrow of a jack-rabbit!'

Billie gazed around him. This was another world from what he had been used to. Ploughed fields and rows of maize and turnips and greens was what he knew about country ways. A distant growl made him start.

'What in hell's that?'

'A cougar quarrelin' over a kill. There's a few up there. Mostly they keep to the higher ground but if they're hungry and food scarce, they come down. Trapper's scared a few off, mostly in winter.'

Billie looked reproachfully at him. 'You said the

other day a cat could have got Sarah!'

'Well, iffen an old crippled 'un had come this way and couldn't catch anythin' on the run, then he would have tackled her. You always have to be on the watch.'

They moved on and Billie improved so much that they got near to a grazing deer before it raised its head in alarm and crashed through the undergrowth at great speed.

'I've never been so close as that to a deer before,' Billie gasped.

'You're lucky it wasn't a stag in ruttin' mood, or he would have charged us! Now we'll just foller him and see if there's a whole heap of 'em. We might get a young 'un.'

Billie followed behind Elijah Joe as they made their way carefully through the thick brush. It was tiring work and Billie was sweating with the exertion of humping the shotgun and a leather bag containing extra ammunition along with a canteen of water and a hunk of bread and some of the old man's pemmican cut up in thick slices.

The tree and brushwood thinned out and they found themselves on a hillside overlooking a valley. To Billie's amazement, the valley floor was covered in milling mustangs. He drew in a sharp breath. He would never have dreamed there were so many wild horses in one place.

'Am I seeing things or are all those horses down there?'

Elijah Joe was scanning them keenly.

'Mmm, I've seen 'em before. It's one of their yearly roundups. Now I wonder why they're panicking? There's somethin' goin' on down there. I bet it's those pesky bronc-busters upsettin' them. Come on, we'll go down and take a look-see.'

Billie scrambled after the old man who'd set off at a trot.

'Dang it,' he was muttering, 'if only we'd brought the hosses!'

'What can we do?' puffed Billie from behind.

'God knows, but I can put a bullet up someone's arse if I catch 'em,' said Elijah Joe fiercely. 'If someone's down there catchin' hosses, I want to know!'

They scrambled down into the lush green pasture, watching the animals suddenly start throwing up heads and neighing and calling for their young.

They saw the beginning of a stampede and Elijah Joe cursed.

'Goddammit! Somethin's spookin' 'em.' Without more ado he cocked his long-range Winchester rifle. He glanced at Billie. 'That gun's ready to pop, so pull the trigger when I say when.'

Billie's adam's apple popped up and down and he gulped. 'Yes sir!' He hoped it wouldn't be necessary.

Then he watched the old man charge ahead. The silly old fool looked as if he was running straight into the nearest bunch.

The horses started to stampede. Billie watched

their graceful movements as with heads up and tails flying, they covered the ground and the pounding of hooves came as a mighty roar. There were all sizes of mustangs of all colours, roans, duns, bays, and blacks with a silvered sheen in the early evening light, chestnuts. Then Billie caught his breath as he glimpsed the most beautiful wonderful golden brown with a cream mane and tail. He'd heard of palominos but never hoped to see a mustang showing the same traits as his noble ancestor.

If I could only catch him, thought Billie in wonderment. Then beside the great stallion he saw a running mare and beside her a foal with the same light mane and tail but with the short stocky body of the Indian paint and the cream and brown markings of a paint.

The sight of the foal fired Billie with an ambition to own such a horse. It was beautiful and it kept up with its galloping mother as the rush went on. For Billie it was but one glimpse, then it and the palomino stallion were gone.

Two gunshots came from the far left and the horses veered away. Elijah Joe cursed and stopped to draw breath.

'I knew it! Those assholes are back and they'll be after my palomino herd! I thought I'd put 'em off when I winged their boss! Come on, let's see what they're up to.' He staggered on while Billie followed. They entered a stand of trees half-way up the other side of the valley and watched from a distance. They could see men on horseback but also in the distance they saw brushwood gathered together to make a woven fence.

Elijah Joe leaned against a tree, his heart thumping from the exertion. Billie feared he could collapse.

'Take it easy, old man or you'll have a heart attack!'

'Not me, son. There's plenty of mileage in me yet. D'you see what they're doin'? They're trying to pen some of them there hosses into that draw yonder! If they do that, then they can take 'em out at leisure! God! I wish I had some sticks of dynamite! I'd show them!'

Billie watched the fleeing horses. 'There's a feller down there riding on their right turning 'em in. Could we go down there and raise merry hell with our guns and turn 'em again?'

Elijah Joe looked at Billie with approval. He smiled. 'Why didn't I think of that? We could scatter 'em. Some would go one way and some another and by the looks of things they're short-handed. They'll have a job controlling 'em.'

Abe cursed as he zigzagged through the brush to urge on the stragglers who'd taken off to hide. There were yearlings and foals who'd lost their mothers with a few mares who'd refused to leave their suckling foals. It took all his time to keep them moving on but he had managed it. I'm like a goddamned sheepdog he grumbled to himself. He was more used to riding flank and keeping up with the leaders but Linx was the boss and this was his job.

He heard the crack of gunfire and realized that something was up. The boss wouldn't use gunfire unless the leaders were making for the open plain. If that happened, they might as well kiss the mustangs goodbye. They might never again have the chance to come upon such massed herds. Abe cursed and waved his hat to encourage the stragglers to run.

Ned, on the right flank, trying to control the turning leaders in their mad rush to the right, wondered what was going on. What in hell was the matter with the beasts? Something or someone was out yonder spooking the bastards. He wondered fleetingly if the Carradine brothers were dumb enough to show themselves as the leaders approached the draw. If they were, then they could only blame themselves if the whole herd charged and bypassed the opening to the boxed-in draw.

Then suddenly before him he glimpsed a kneeling figure, high on the hillside. The sonofabitch was aiming a long-range rifle into the air and Abe recognized the sound of Spencer fire. So that was the goddamned bastard who'd fired at Hank and dropped him and now the interfering maverick was spooking the hosses!

He risked a pot-shot of his own and saw the man duck and roll away. A puff of dust and smoke rose barely feet away from the man and Abe knew his shot had been close. That'll teach the sonofabitch to interfere, Abe thought grimly.

But the damage was done. His own shot sent the stragglers into a headlong panic. They thundered after the main herd.

God damn it to hell! Ned muttered to himself and pulled up his horse. No need to wear the poor beast out on a futile effort that would get them nowhere.

He rode disconsolately behind, breathing in dust raised by the stampeding herd.

He saw Linx trotting towards him through the hazy atmosphere.

'What in hell happened?' bawled Linx. The pounding of hooves was now growing fainter.

'They were deliberately spooked, boss, by the man who downed Hank. I recognized his gunfire.'

'Was it that big gorilla trapper, Barnaby Dougan?'

'Not him. Could have been one of his men, but it was a long-range Spencer he had, whoever he was.'

'Where did he shoot from?'

'Right over there, just below that stand of trees.'

'Right! We go and get him!'

'Hey, just a minute, boss. What about the Carradines? They'll think we did it.'

Linx nodded. 'Now that's a thought. We'd better round up Abe and see what he's up to and then sort out the Carradines once and for all.'

They found Abe 'sheepherding' a few yearlings

and a couple of suckling mares with running foals.They were exhausted with running and now stood in a huddle as they had no leader to turn to in this time of trouble.

Abe grinned at them. 'Lost the sumbitches, eh? Well, if it's any consolation we've got two mares and eight young 'uns. better than nothin', boss!'

'You did better than us, Abe. Some busy bee spooked the lot and they'll be miles away by now.' Linx looked the animals over critically. 'Not a bad bunch. The mares look good.' He looked around him and saw that they were near the stream that ran through the little valley. He dismounted and took off his saddle and bridle and rubbed down the horse with a fragrant bunch of sagebrush. 'There, that should fix him, no smell of human on him now. Go on, boy, take those mares and foals down to water!' He slapped the horse's rump. The horse lifted his head and neighed and trotted forward, his back legs coming up in an exuberance of freedom.

The mares twitched ears and watched and then warily moved forward to follow suit. They were used to following a stallion and now the mares followed by the foals went down to the water and drank.

Linx grinned.

'I learned that trick from an old Mex. Now while they're busy, we'll erect a rope barrier from the cliff there, to the big boulder yonder and then we'll fill the gaps with brushwood. Now look lively, fellers!'

The rope was soon slung and the brushwood was

to hand. A makeshift fence was soon erected around the unsuspecting mustangs.

A broad strip of lush grass covered the banks of the stream, which the beasts cropped contentedly seeming unaware of their lack of freedom.

Linx and his men paused in their labours. It was a sight to make any bronc-buster's heart swell. The next job would be cutting out the mares, wrestling them until they tired, then getting hackamores, which were looped bridles, over their heads and into their mouths.

Then would come the patient mastering and gentling of the animals until they lost their fear. Some mustangs fought long and hard before the first act of taming. Others meekly allowed the ropes to be attached and stood quivering and waiting for the next move. Those mares with young foals could be vicious and they had to be hobbled and brought to their knees with several men holding them with ropes. It was all in the day's work. These two should be a doddle.

But one of them was an eye-flashing biting she-devil. She was a black beauty and reared, using her front hooves like a boxer. She kicked out at the back end, and Abe caught a glancing blow to the ribs while trying to hobble her.

He grunted and cursed as all three men strove to quieten her.

'You all right?' Linx called with some concern. It wasn't usually Abe and Ned who participated in this operation. It took all the strength of the younger men to quell panic-stricken horses. Linx knew what a calamity it would be here out in the wilds if a man had his ribs stove in or a broken leg.

'I'll do,' grunted Abe, trying to ignore the pain, having had the breath punched out of him.

Finally, the mare quietened when Linx allowed her foal to come to her. Linx took off his Stetson and wiped his brow on his shirt-sleeve.

'She's a good 'un. I'll break her in for myself. She's got spunk and staying power.' He looked the other mare over. She'd been little trouble and now stood quiet with her foal nuzzling her underbelly.

'What about the Carradines? They'll want them both.'

'Oh, to hell with them. If they catch up with us, we'll be ready for them.'

But they weren't.

Linx and the boys were relaxing and and figuring on how to find their way to their own camp when suddenly the Carradine bunch were surrounding them, even Luke, who looked on with a vacuous grin and a shotgun waving dangerously about stood with Tilly a little behind the others.

Tucker strode forward, an evil grin on his thin face. He looked dangerous, trigger-happy.

Linx looked helplessly around at them all and he reckoned each and every one of them was wild enough and savage enough to kill at the least provocation. They were loco the lot of them!

'Were you thinkin' of makin' a break, mister? You sure made a good job of spookin' those hosses!'

'Hey now, we spooked no hosses! We're in the business of catchin' 'em not panickin' the sumbitches into runnin' into the next county! That way butters no parsnips!'

Tucker looked doubtful and glanced at his brothers, while Tilly swung her hips, eyes gleaming.

'Can I have one of 'em now, Tucker?'

Tucker waved her back impatiently. 'Tilly, remember what I told you. Go cool your arse off in the stream or somethin'. This is men's talk.'

Tilly pouted. 'You don't need 'em all just to talk!'

'Tilly!' he bellowed warningly and then gestured to Jed Carradine. 'Take the hot little bitch and dunk her in the stream!' Jed snatched the shotgun from her hand and caught her by her wrists as she wrestled him to get away.

She screamed and yelled and punched at Jed while young Luke looked on grinning, thinking it was all some game.

'Luke,' she screamed, 'hit Jed with that gun, he's hurtin' me!'

Luke suddenly looked frightened, not sure of what he should do. Saliva dribbled from his mouth and he began to cry.

'Luke!' Tilly screamed again but now she was being hauled away, turning and twisting as Jed dragged her swearing and cursing to the bank of the stream.

As Jed threw her into a deep pool Linx sprang to his feet with a good old-fashioned Rebel yell and grabbed the gun that Tucker had unwittingly let fall as he watched the battle between brother and sister.

Ned sprang after Linx and Abe followed more slowly, still suffering from the mustang's kick. But his gun was aimed just as firmly on Bill Carradine while Ned went after Jed and brought back a drenched and shivering Tilly with a bewildered Jed who couldn't believe how quickly the balance of power had changed.

'What do we do with 'em, boss?' Ned asked.

'Get your rope, Ned, and we'll string 'em all together and leave 'em.'

'What about the girl?'

'Her too. Leave her free and she'll have our balls for breakfast!'

So Linx, with gun at the ready, watched as Abe and Ned strung them all like a line of horses with a spitting kicking Tilly on the end. Then they tied what was left of the rope around a tree and took away knives and guns and threw them into the stream.

Linx walked around the little bunch, whose wrists were knotted tight. Luke cried and Linx felt a touch of remorse. The poor little bastard didn't know what was happening to them all. But he hardened his heart. They deserved what they got.

'When we get free, we'll hunt you down if it takes for ever!' Tucker Carradine raved.

'Aw, shut it! Think yourselves lucky we didn't fill you up with lead!' Linx spat back. 'When you get free, we'll be long gone!'

There was no time to rest. Linx deemed it wiser to make for their own camp. He looked at the small herd they'd captured. It would be a shame to leave them behind.

He took a chance. They used the hackamores and hobbling ropes on the two untamed mares, with extra ropes on the back legs only to use if absolutely necessary. A pull on these ropes and the mares could be felled on to their sides at the first sign of rebellion. In all other ways they were going to close-herd the two so that their own foals would tag along and in doing so would encourage the other yearlings to follow their instincts and trail behind.

They had used this trick before and unless the young herd was spooked, it could be successful.

Quickly they left the valley and retraced their steps towards the direction they expected to find their own camp.

The foals were docile and after a couple of skirmishes with the two mares, they succeeded at moving along at a slow rate.

It was Ned's horse who, pricking up his ears, warned them that something or someone was in the undergrowth. Ned drew his gun. He had visions of a bunch of Dougan's hardcases sneaking up on them and was surprised when an old man and a youth stepped out of the tangle of bushes on to the trail.

Around the boy's neck was slung the carcass of a young deer. Ned's eyes narrowed as he saw the Spencer long-range rifle that the old man was pointing so significantly at Ned's belly. So this could be the son of a bitch who shot Hank.

Linx and Abe's attention was taken up with watching the two mares.

'Boss, we got company!' Ned bawled and Linx looked around, plain startled.

'Hell!' Ned heard him mutter.

Elijah Joe looked the mustangs over. He was angry. The mares were trembling and sweating and he didn't like the way the beasts were being close-herded and the rope lines holding them. He raised the rifle higher.

'You be the varmints chasin' the mustangs?'

'Yep,' answered Linx, 'and you be the bastard who shot my partner?'

Elijah Joe nodded.

'I don't hold with hoss punchers comin' into God's own country and takin' what ain't theirs!'

'You kill deer,' Linx pointed out, nodding over at the deer slung about Billie's shoulders.

'One deer for food, friend, not takin' a whole mess of animals.'

Linx shrugged.

'It's a free country, mister. What's your beef? There's thousands of wild mustangs. A few here and there, it's the same as cullin'.'

'No it ain't. Cullin' means takin' the oldsters or

the lame ones. You've got yorselves some prime animals, the next generation you might say. I don't hold with that.'

'Who d'you think you are? God? What right have you to come gabbin' like a preacher?'

'Look, mister, I live in these parts. That small herd you were chasin' were special to me. I watched them foals grow up and mate and have foals of their own. They're my family, see?'

'Iffen they're family why didn't you close-herd 'em?'

'Because they fare better wild and free. That palomino you was chasin' is mine. I'm waitin' for a foal just like him.'

'Then you're no different from the likes of us, friend, so quit yor high-falutin' drivel!'

'You watch yor mouth! I don't like yor attitude. Now, as a peace offerin' I think you should cut those mustangs free.'

'Like hell we will!' Linx answered sharply. Elijah Joe raised his weapon threateningly.

'I say you will!'

'Just try and make us and see where it gets you! Those Carradine bastards couldn't hold us and neither will you!'

Elijah Joe let his gun droop.

'You had a run in with the Carradines?'

'Yep, and we left the bastards tied up to a tree. They're loco, the lot of 'em includin' that hot-arsed sister of theirs!'

'You saw Tilly?' Elijah Joe was looking interested now. 'It's a wonder you got away alive. She's a real tigress!'

'Tied her up good and proper with the rest of the litter.'

'Well now, if you can beat that mangy lot, then there must be some good in you! How about comin' back to my place and sharin' some of this here deer?' He nodded in Billie's direction. Billie, who had stood silently by while this discussion was going on, gave a nod of agreement. The deer was making his neck ache. He wanted to move on.

Linx considered the offer. 'Maybe we could discuss this business of the mustangs more amicably over some grub?'

'Yeh, well, I suppose those mares and foals aren't goin' to hurt the herds none. They ain't from my herd anyway. I know each and every one of the palomino's band.'

'We could help you catch the palomino stallion if you want him,' Linx offered now that the tension had eased.

'Thanks, mister, but I don't want the stallion caught. I'll bide my time and get a foal from him. It would be a crime to catch such a splendid free spirit! But come on then, let's be on our way. Billie, lead on, boy.'

'What about the mares and foals? Will they be safe from the Dougans?'

Elijah Joe frowned. 'You come up against them?'

'Yeh. The Carradines got the drop on us and wanted us to help smoke 'em out from their roost. We're not gunhawks, we're bronc-busters so we lit out.'

' 'Pears to me you got big trouble in these 'ere parts iffen you got both the Dougans and the Carradines gunnin' for you, mister. I sure wouldn't like to be in yor boots!' Elijah Joe shook his head and tutted. 'But come away. Those beasts will be safe enough where they are for now. It'll not be too far from where I roost.'

The three men dowsed their own small fire, scattered the dead embers and packed up their gear. Soon they were all on their way.

They left the main trail and followed a little-trod deer path and soon they were climbing out of the woodland and up into the foothills. Soon they came to the small stream that meandered and ran shallowly over the stones before the soddy that Elijah Joe called home came into view.

There was no sign of Sarah and the fire was long dead. Elijah Joe squatted down and touched the embers which were barely warm. Billie threw down the carcass and ran into the soddy.

'Sarah! Where are you? For God's sake, what's happened?' He ran out, eyes staring and panic-stricken.

'She's not here, Elijah Joe. What's happened to her?'

Elijah Joe stood up, eyes narrowed. 'And there's

no sign of Trapper.' He looked about him and saw that his wooden bucket was missing. 'Mebbe she's down by the stream takin' a bath or somethin' and hasn't heard us. Go on, Billie, you take a look-see.'

But he looked worriedly at Linx and the two men. 'There's somethin' wrong. Trapper would have heard us and come runnin''.

Billie ran back with the empty bucket. 'She's gone, Elijah Joe, and Trapper's been shot. He's away back in the undergrowth. There looks to have been a mighty fight before the wolf got shot. There's blood all over the grass and stones!'

Elijah Joe raised his fist heavenwards, sparkling tears in his old eyes.

'The Dougan bastards! They've found her, Billie. That's where she is. With those goddamn bastards and God help her if we don't get her away from them in the next few hours!'

SIX

Ed Gittens and Paddy O'Rourke drew rein. Ed raised his Stetson and wiped sweat from his brow. The sun beat down and both men felt the need to dismount and allow their mounts to drink at the small stream in front of them. Paddy O'Rourke spat.

'I sure am choked.' He looked at the sun overhead. 'What say if we build a fire and have us some coffee and chow? We've hunted this country up hill and down dale and never a hint of Linx and the boys.'

'It's too soon to return to camp. What you think happened to 'em, Paddy?' said Ed as he dismounted, his horse already stretching for water at the stream's edge.

'I dunno. Must have gone further up the mountain. Mebbe we should take a look where that gap is yonder, but we'll eat first. My guts think my throat's cut!'

They took their time, making a small fire and resting while the battered tin coffee-pot boiled.

They rifled saddle-bags for some of Jake's panbread and generously cut slices of salt bacon. When replete, they sat back, leaning against a tall pine tree, put their hats over their faces and slept.

A woman's scream startled them both awake. Confused, the sound came like the wail of a banshee and the superstitious Paddy sat upright clutching hat and gun.

'By all the Holy Saints, what's that?' he said, turning a suddenly ashen face to Ed who was listening intently.

'Sounds like one of the big cats has caught himself a meal,' he began when the sound came again. 'By hell, no! It do sound like a woman in trouble!'

'A woman in trouble? Naw, how can it be? To me, it sounds like the Devil himself wrestlin' one of his demons! Sure and begorra, it must be a soul in torment!'

'I tell you it's a woman!' Ed got to his feet, reaching for his rifle and cocking it before moving further into the bushes that led away from the stream. 'I tell you there's somethin' out there and it ain't no spirit! Come on, or are you too yeller-livered to take a look-see?'

Paddy, angered by Ed's remark, cursed under his breath and bounded up, grabbing at his rifle and also easing his Colt from its holster. Whether it was a human cry or the wailing of a soul in hell, he could show the bastard that he wasn't afraid and could shoot straight.

They moved forward together. There were no birds twittering and it was as if the woodlands were listening. Paddy began to sweat.

'I don't like it,' he began, when the scream came again and Paddy jumped. But this time it seemed nearer and there were muffled sounds of fighting. Ed stepped forward on light feet, his arm waving Paddy back as he parted the bushes to look on an open glade. He watched and let out a gasp. 'Holy shit!' he murmured.

Paddy blundering behind him whispered, 'What is it?'

Ed grunted. 'Look for yourself.'

Paddy looked and gulped, for there were three men grouped about a woman. Two were holding her down by her wrists and ankles as she struggled desperately to free herself while the third man was undoing his belt.

'Jesus, Mary and Joseph!' Paddy crossed himself. 'The spalpeens are going to rape her!'

'Not if we can help her!' Ed coolly took aim and fired at the man whose pants were now round his ankles. He yelped and turned swiftly, falling over himself as he did so. The other two men straightened up quickly and went for their guns.

Paddy's rifle crashed out and as it recoiled, hitting his shoulder, he saw the man he'd aimed at bounce back into the air as if he'd been punched in the chest. A gout of red blood stained his front.

Ed took a shot at the third man and missed, as

the man dived for the bushes and was gone.

The first man was now scrabbling for his gun and was still on the ground when he took a pot-shot at Ed. Ed heard the whistle of the bullet as it passed him. It sounded like an angry hornet.

Then the man was scrambling away into the bushes and the girl was lying alone.

She groaned as the two men came warily towards her, expecting shots to come from the bushes. But none came.

Ed crouched down beside the girl. Her bodice was torn and her full rounded breasts drew his eyes. Then he forced himself to look at her. She would have been pretty but for the ugly bruising on her cheeks and the bleeding cut on her mouth. She had a lopsided look as her right cheek and jaw swelled visibly.

Her long hair straggled like rats' tails. Ed wasn't sure what he should do. Paddy elbowed him aside.

'I'll look after her. You watch and see if those goddamn sons of bitches come back.'

He glanced coolly at the man lying some feet away who didn't move, then gathered the girl in his arms. He felt for his flask, then touched her lips with the rotgut whiskey.

She choked on the strong liquor, fluttered her eyes and then looked up at him, suddenly wary and frightened. She tried to struggle, then groaned.

'It's all right, miss, you're safe. We won't hurt you.'

Dazedly she looked at him.

'Who're you?' she managed to utter from swollen lips.

'I'm Paddy O'Rourke and that is my pard, Ed Gittens and we're lookin' for our boss, Linx Firman and two of our crew. We're in these here parts to hunt mustangs.'

The girl struggled to sit up, suddenly conscious of her state of undress. She blushed and tried to pull the strips of torn cloth to cover herself.

'Did they. . . ? I mean . . . did they. . . ?' And she looked down at herself, suddenly confused but Paddy knew what she was trying to say. She could only shake her head in embarrasment.

'No, miss. We heard you scream and you sure fought hard. It took two of 'em to hold you down, begorra, and the third was just gettin' down to . . . er . . . you know what, when we surprised the fornicatin' bastards. May they rot in hell!'

'Oh!' The girl turned her face away and Paddy saw the deep blush which covered her cheeks and neck. He felt awkward.

'Have another pull at my flask, miss. It'll put new heart into you.'

She shook her head. 'Thank you, but no. I never take strong drink.'

'All the more reason to do so now. It will cure the shivers and the shock you have suffered.'

But Sarah was adamant.

Suddenly she started to shake. She put her head

into her hands and started to cry. Paddy looked at Ed. Neither man knew how to cope with females who cried.

'Er . . . miss, if you would just take another drink?' Paddy offered. 'Calm yor nerves, like?'

'*No*! Just leave me alone!' She sprang up and started to run in a distracted headlong bolt. A few minutes more and she would have been lost in the woodland.

'Hey! Wait a minute!' Paddy shouted and then cursed as Sarah, hysterical and past reasoning, ran on.

'Goddammit! We'll have to get after her,' Paddy gasped and started to pound after the distraught girl, tearing through bushes and cactus which tore at his clothes and brought blood to the scratches on his arms.

He found her on the ground, crying and beating the earth. She'd tripped over a root and she turned a terrified face to his.

'Please . . . don't hurt me. . . .' Her eyes were wild and unseeing.

Paddy cursed the men who'd shocked the reason out of her. If he got them in his sights he'd kill them like so much vermin.

He raised her up. She was trembling like some wild animal.

'Calm yourself,' he said again. 'If you tell us your name and where you live, we'll take you to your folk.'

She stared at him and as he watched the light of

reason gradually came back into her eyes. She drooped and he held her from sinking to the ground. It was as if all her strength and energy had left her and she was like a helpless rag doll.

'I . . . I . . . I'm Sarah Crayshaw . . . and I'm all alone except for Billie,' she began in a faint voice.'My pa . . .' She broke down again and Paddy made soothing noises.

'What about yor pa?'

'Those horrible men killed him. We were driving through the pass when we were set upon. Billie got away.' She sniffled and wiped her nose on the shreds of her blouse, then held the bits about her to make herself respectable.

'What happened then?'

'They took me up into the mountains. There's a place up there where there's women and children. They're like wild beasts!'

'Then how come you're here?'

'Billie followed and saved me. The Dougans had a fight with some other mountain men and we got away. I was shot and an old man found us and looked after us. He saved my life.'

'Then how come those men got hold of you?'

'Elijah Joe and Billie went off hunting and left me alone. The men came. I think they saw our fire.'

'They should never have left you alone!' Paddy was quite indignant.

'Elijah Joe had a tame wolf who stayed with me. They thought I should be safe with him. But the men shot him after a fight. Trapper tore one of the men's arms and then he was shot.'

'Then they dragged you away, so you can't be far from this old man's camp?'

'No. It lies somewhere over there.' Sarah pointed towards the west.

'Then what are we waiting for? We'll take you back.' Paddy offered her his jerkin to cover herself. 'There you are, miss,' he said roughly. 'You'll feel better if you're covered up!'

He hoisted her on to his horse while Ed stood silently by, then Paddy sprang up behind. He felt awkward as her warm body leaned back against him.

Suddenly he was full of fury at the men who had laid hands on her. He scowled at Ed who was looking at him a bit quizzically.

'What you lookin' at, buster? To be sure and begorra, cain't a feller do somethin' decent for once without you kinda smirkin'?'

Billie looked at Elijah Joe in despair.

'The bastards must have taken her back to their roost? We'll have to go up there. . . .'

'Now, now, don't go half-cocked, young 'un,' Linx said quietly as Abe and Ned stretched their legs and wiped sweaty foreheads. 'We've ranged all the way south. Maybe they're restin' up somewheres. They could be anywhere.'

'They'll take her back . . .'

'Not before they have their way with her,' Ned cut

in brutally and Billie paled. 'Stands to reason, don't it? They'll want first go before the other fellers get their hands on her. God help her!'

'Jesus!' Billie turned away so that they couldn't see the sudden tears flowing. He was fond of Sarah and she'd always been the young innocent to be watched over and protected. Old Tot Crayshaw would rise up from wherever he was, if he knew how his daughter was being violated!

'Look, there's no good in goin' further on empty stomachs and no use imagining what's happened to the lass,' Linx said prosaically. 'We gotta keep up our strength and then make plans. If they've taken her up to their roost, then they won't have harmed her beyond havin' their way with her. Now don't look like that, boy. There's many a woman been raped and survived it. It's not the end of the world!'

'How can you say that?' Billie yelled. 'You didn't know her like I did. She was good and chaste . . .'

'Christ! They all are at some time in their lives, boy! Be yor age! She's lucky it was white men who took her! They could have been Indians. Have you thought of that? Then we would never get her back!'

Billie was struck dumb. Elijah Joe spat on the dry ground.

'Come on, we'll make tracks and go back and roast that deer and fill our bellies and we'll have us some whiskey with our coffee and it might put some cheer into this 'ere boy.'

They were nearing Elijah Joe's artfully concealed

soddy when the old man paused and lifted a hand warningly.

'What is it?' Billie whispered loud enough for Elijah Joe to hear.

'Shut yor damn mouth! There's some son of a bitch moochin' round!' Elijah Joe cocked his rifle while Linx and the two men did the same. Then they all inched forward, making sure none of the horses shook a bridle or whinnied.

Then Elijah Joe took a chance and aimed for his grass-grown soddy roof. A bullet whined and pinged while turf and dirt erupted up into the trees.There was a scream from inside the soddy and they saw a couple of rifles poking through two slits in the rough log wall at each side of the small doorway.

'Whoever you are, stand back or as sure as hell we'll blast you all to Kingdom Come, that we will an' all an' all!'

Paddy's rich brogue filled the air.

Abe and Ned started and Linx swore. They knew that voice. They couldn't mistake that voice.

'Paddy!' roared Linx, 'It's us! Put yor gun down, you mad sonofabitch!'

'Linx? Is that you?' They all saw the sudden movement in the darkness of the doorway, and Paddy and Ed cautiously appeared, guns at the ready, fearing some trickery.

'Of course, it's me, dumbhead! Me and Abe and Ned and we're with the old man and some young kid. Is the girl with you?'

Paddy and Ed eased out of the doorway, grinning.

'By hell, it is! Thank God you're here, boss!'

'The girl, Paddy. What about the girl!'

'Oh, shook up, some. We come across three fellers indulgin' theirselves but we give 'em different ideas. Two got away but there's a dead 'un lyin' in the undergrowth.'

Billie ran forward, entered the soddy and found Sarah lying on the makeshift bed. He was horrified at what he saw. She smiled up at him through swollen lips.

'Billie, I'm glad you're back. Those men saved me. . .' Her voice was a whisper.

'Who did it, Sarah?'

'It was some of the Dougan gang. I recognized them. They shot Trapper too. He tried to fight them off.' She started to cry again.

Billie gathered her in his arms and held her close.

'You're safe now, Sarah. Don't cry. Just rest yorself and leave them to us!'

Outside, Linx and the two older men and Elijah Joe were listening to Ed and Paddy's account of the action.

'You say two of them got away?' Elijah Joe scowled and shook his head. 'A very bad business. They'll be back, especially now that they know the location of this place.' He whistled through blackened rotting teeth. 'A very bad business. I don't like it.'

Linx walked up and down, thinking. Then he turned round and pointed to the dead fire.

'Let's eat and think on it. Ed, rustle up some dry wood and make a fire. Paddy, you butcher this deer, while Billie, you see to the horses then get the makings for the coffee and get crackin' with the fryin' pan, while Elijah Joe and you two fellers help me to come up with a sound plan of action.'

Elijah Joe looked at Linx with shrewd eyes.

'Shouldn't we fort up and wait for the bastards comin'?'

'Naw. The less they know about this place the better for you. We go to them!'

'Jesus! How do we do that?'

'Let's eat first. I think better on a full belly.' Linx deliberately sat down with the older men around him. He leant his head on his still warm saddle, hunkered down, put his hat over his head and shut his eyes.

While they were eating Linx announced part of his plan.

'First thing, we go back to Hank and our camp.'

'But Hank and Charlie ain't in no fit state . . .' objected Abe and got a forkful of venison waved in front of his eyes.

'I know that, dumbhead! But Jake has all his faculties and he's no mean hand with dynamite!'

Abe and Ned stared at Linx, fascinated.

'Dynamite? What you want that for? I know Jake carries dynamite in the stores for blockin' draws and gullies when needed but how do we use it on the Dougans?'

'We don't.' Linx champed on a mouthful of venison.

'But what *do* we do with it?'

'We go after those mustangs and we chase 'em back to that valley and we help 'em along with some well-placed sticks. Two should be enough to send the herd flyin' and when they're inside, we'll seal 'em in, and let 'em trample the lot!'

Abe stared at Linx with horror.

'We cain't do that! What about the women and kids?'

'The Carradines want women and they know another way in. If they want women they can damn well go get 'em! That way,' he said turning to Elijah Joe, 'will keep 'em off yor back!'

Elijah Joe slowly nodded and then grinned. 'They'll be too taken up with their new women to bother me none. Yes, I like it!'

Just then, Sarah appeared at the open door of the soddy. She made her way, staggering a little and limping to come towards the flickering fire.

'I . . . I think I can eat something now,' she began, and Billie got up to help her settle beside them. He poured coffee into a tin mug and loaded her plate with meat. Linx noted her bruised and swollen face and felt a great anger stir within him. He'd make sure not one damn member of the Dougan camp got away. He swallowed his coffee, and tossed away the dregs, then stood up and left the group. He walked away into the outer darkness to complete his plan.

They would have to conciliate the Carradines and find out how much time would be needed for them to raid the camp at night and take the womenfolk and kids away. There would also have to be a diversion to give the Carradines enough time to persuade the women to leave.

He scratched his head. It would have to be good.

Abe and Ned joined him.

'You think this idea of yours will work?'

'Why not? We'll take 'em by surprise.'

'But the Carradines? They're as dangerous as the Dougans!' Ned said doubtfully. Linx laughed.

'The dangerous bit will be puttin' it over to them. When the idea sinks in that women could be at stake, they'll go along with it. If you were starved of women, wouldn't you?'

'Yeh, if I was their age, I sure would,' Ned agreed but Abe still scowled.

'It's a big risk if it all goes wrong.'

'What other plan can we come up with?' Linx asked sharply. 'What d'you think we should do? We can't leave those murderin' bastards free range for ever!' Abe shrugged.

'I ain't got no ideas, boss. I'm just a bronc-buster and I like a quiet life.'

'Then dry up and shut up! What I want is a diversion. Something that will send the Dougans half-cocked while the Carradines get in there and get the women and kids out.'

'We could do with a band of Indians on the prod.

You know . . . singin' and ghost dancin' and raisin' merry hell with a lot of whoopin' and screamin',' Ned suggested with a grin.

But Linx didn't laugh.

'You might have got somethin' there, bub. We could do some mighty fine yellin' and would sound like Indians at a distance. It would certainly bring Dougan and his boys down to investigate.'

Elijah Joe grinned. 'I have a war-drum and I know the Apache medicine chant to bring good luck. It makes the blood run cold and the heart shrivel!'

'You do? How come?' Linx was curious.

'I was kidnapped by the Apache as a young boy and I learned their ways. I became one of them until I was taken again by white men.' He sounded bitter as he went on, 'The preacher who took me in hand regarded me as a wild animal. He beat me. Called me a barbarian because I was not brought up as a Christian. White folk have the hard stony heart!'

'Hey! Wait a minute, we're not all the same. What happened to the preacher?'

'I killed him and took to the mountains. You are the first white men and she's the first white woman I have had much to do with.'

And do you regret this?'

Elijah Joe shrugged and spat on the ground.

'Yes and no. You have brought trouble but you also have brought a new experience. I find not all white men are like that preacher. It will be lonely when you move on.'

He said the last words proudly but with a poignancy that touched Sarah.

'You could come with us, especially now your wolf is dead.' She smiled at him. 'I must thank you for caring for me when I needed help.'

He shook his head. 'This is my home. I will never leave it, but I shall help you rid these mountains of a bunch of criminals who poison the very earth they tread.'

'Good. Then you will tell us what we should do to distract these men.'

'There will be a smudge fire to build, down in a hollow so that it can be located easily in the darkness. There will be chantin' and Apache war yells and the drum beatin' its message in the background. The chantin' in a singsong will be heard for a great distance. There will be a lull between rituals. That is usual. Durin' the lulls we move away and surround the sacred fire and when the Dougans come, we greet them with bullets.'

'You mean we should have a shoot-out there and then?'

'No. We fire to frighten and confuse. The chantin' will come from the north and south and east and west. They will think it is ghost chantin' and the wailin' of dead Apache.'

Linx drew a deep breath.

'And how in hell do we do all that?'

'We split into two lots. First we do it all together to attract their attention. Then we split and the first lot chant in the north while the others get ready and answer the chant in the south. Then everyone moves like snakes in the grass and again come the calls but in east and west. Sound rebounds at night. They won't know what hits them.'

'Meanwhile the Carradines will get the women away from their prison? If they'll play along.'

'They will. I know the Carradines. They need women and they also need horses. They'll probably take over Dougan's place which is better than where they live. Oh, yes, they'll play along.'

'So the first thing we do is get back to camp and Hank and put our plans to him. We need Jake along for his dynamite skills. He was once a miner and knows exactly how much and when to use it.'

'What about Sarah? We can't leave her alone here,' Paddy asked.

'I could stay with her,' offered Billie.

'No, we need all hands on this caper. We'll take her to Hank and he'll look after her.'

'But . . .' Billie protested.

'Billie,' interrupted Sarah, 'Linx is right. You're needed with them. I'll manage. I'll stay in their camp. I'll be fine, sure I will.' She gave a lopsided smile, her face still too bruised and painful.

'Right! Then that's settled. Paddy, you take Sarah to Hank and we'll go and see what's happened to the Carradines and then we'll all meet back at the camp.'

SEVEN

Tucker Carradine cursed as he struggled against the ropes that bound him. Tilly was crying and his brothers, all connected by Linx Firman's rope which Abe and Ned had used to tie them all to the base of the cottonwood tree, strove to free themselvs but only pulled the knots tighter.

'Jesus! I'll string those bastards up by the balls when I get free!' raved Tucker.

'When we get free,' Jed panted as he pulled against Bill Carradinc in his efforts to get some play on his wrist rope.

Tilly raised her voice to a scream.

'Tucker, do somethin'. M' wrist's swellin'!'

'How the hell can I, you stupid bitch?'

The struggle seemed to have gone on for hours and all of them knew the danger of prowling mountain cats and timber wolves.

Suddenly a sound made all hearts pound. Someone or something was moving cautiously through the undergrowth. Tilly whimpered and a harsh whisper told her to stow it. They held their breath and Luke began to snuffle in fear.

Then Ma Carradine, carrying an old-shotgun, broke through the thick bushes, blood running down her cheek from scratches and wearing a torn and filthy skirt and man's jacket. Grey hair flowing free, and a beaverskin hat jammed down tight made her a fiendish sight.

'Ma!' they all howled together and Ma Carradine pursed her lips, drew her heavy eyebrows together and snarled in her intimidating voice.

'How the hell did you all allow yorselves to get corralled like so many hosses? Tucker Carradine, I'm ashamed of you! I thought you of all of 'em had enough brains to keep outa traps!' She fired the shotgun over their heads in temper.

'Look out, Ma, you're gonna kill us!' Jed shouted. 'You're plumb loco!'

'You're the ones who's loco! Lettin' yourselves be took like so many lambs! I suppose it was those god-damn strangers?' As she spoke she was cutting the wrist bonds on Tilly and Luke. 'I've a rare good mind to leave you assholes here all night!'

'Now Ma, don't get in a tizzy,' Bill Carradine pleaded. 'Just cut the crap and loosen us up.'

'Me havin' to come lookin' for you and thinkin' them Dougans had got you and me all alone, not even Tilly and Luke to fetch and carry for me. By God, if I was younger I'd give the lot of you a fair good hidin'!'

She gave Tilly the knife and stood leaning against a tree, a hand on her heart and bellows heaving.

Tilly was sawing through Tucker's bonds when the click of a gun made them all look up.

Linx and the rest of them had crept up on them during Ma's tirade. Now Linx stepped out into the clearing. They had already checked on the mustangs held in the makeshift corral. All were still there, munching grass.

Linx grinned.

'So you had to wait for your old woman to come and rescue you!'

Tucker glared.

'Bastard! I'll kill you when I get free!'

'You and whose army?'

Ma slapped Tucker across the head.

'Stop that roosterin'. You're like a gobblin' turkey cock! What brings you back, mister? You didn't come out of the goodness of yor heart.'

'No, ma'am. We came for yor boys' help.'

'Our help!' Tucker guffawed. 'I'll see you in hell first!' Ma Carradine slapped him again.

'Fool! You're just like yor pa! You ain't no brains, you big dumbhead! What you want help with, mister?'

Ma's younger sons crowded close as they were freed by Tilly. Curious, they wanted to hear what was wanted, especially as they recognized the old man who lived alone.

They looked at Abe and Ned who had their rifles

cocked, ready for action and then at Ed and young Billie who both looked wary.

Linx turned to Tucker. 'How you fancy helpin' us to clear out the Dougan bunch and get yorselves some mustangs into the bargain?'

Tucker's eyes gleamed. 'How you expect to get rid of that bunch? They be mighty hard to shift.'

'You said you knew of another way into that there valley. Was you boastin' or is it so?'

'Yep, we know a road in. It's an old Indian trail, cuts through the mountain yonder. It's an old watercourse, dried up now but for a trickle of water when it rains.'

'If we make a diversion and get the men out of the valley durin' the night hours could you get in there and take out the women and kids?'

Tucker frowned but his eyes gleamed. 'Why should we do that?'

'To save their lives. We don't fight women and kids.'

'You mean you're gonna massacre the whole goddamn bunch?'

'Not us. They'll havta take their chances with the mustangs.'

Tucker stared and the other brothers moved uneasily. Tilly was edging around, eyeing young Billie up and down.

Ma saw her and slapped her hard. 'Give over, Tilly, or I'll tie you to this tree, by God I will!' Tilly sulked and held her flaming cheek. 'I want a man, Ma!'

'All in good time, girl. Now look to Luke and behave yorself!'

'What about the mustangs?'

'We're gonna turn this lot loose and let 'em find the rest of their herd. They'll be hangin' about somewhere nearby and when we do, we'll head 'em up trail towards that gap into Dougan's valley. We'll stampede 'em and those sumbitches can take their chances.'

Tucker laughed.

'You've got some hopes, mister. How d'you know they'll react like you think?'

'They'll come runnin' shit-scared, thinkin' about the womenfolk and kids. What about it, Carradine? Are you with us?'

Tucker shrugged and looked at his brothers for a decision, but it was Ma Carradine who decided for them.

'Of course we'll do it! If the plan succeeds we can take over the valley. Anything's better than the muckhole we live in! Then we'll have horses too. You boys can break 'em in and we can use the old wagon again. Of course we'll do it!'

Linx eyed Tucker. 'How about it, Carradine? Yor ma's for it.'

Abe and Ned and Elijah Joe raised their guns in silent threat. Tucker knew he had no option. He didn't trust these strangers, especially the steely-eyed bossman. But the thought of the Dougan bunch being wiped out, the promise of women and most of all a secure home in a verdant valley with horses to boot, made it sound like paradise. It would get Ma off his back, her grumblings were hard to bear and as for Tilly, that hot-arsed bitch, she might find herself a feller if she could go into town, and they could get rid of her for ever. Maybe Ma would go with her!

That thought spurred him on. After it was all over, then they could deal with these cool hard-eyed strangers. He would never forgive the indignity of being left roped up and helpless.

'Yeh, I go along with it.' He smiled at Linx but there was no warmth to it. He reminded Linx of a coyote baring his teeth for battle.

'Good,' Linx replied. 'Now this is the way we do it.'

Night had fallen. Barnaby Dougan lounged near the communal camp-fire which was always burning, night and day. The sullen womenfolk cooked together and gossiped while the few children played nearby. It was the centre of the small community. Around the fire at a distance were crude log cabins, built wherever a man chose without thought for any kind of regularity. A few had small patches of garden which the women managed.

The women varied. There were several squaws as well as white women. A couple who were the elders ruled them all. There was a certain pecking order. The newcomers, unwilling victims of kidnap, being the slaves of those taken earlier.

There was much resentment between the women as the newcomers usually ousted the older women from their menfolk. But all had one thing in common. They all wanted to be free.

Now Barnaby sat back with his cronies. This was the time he liked best. Belly filled, chores done, and the night stretching ahead. It was time to dull the senses with the homemade beer, talk of exploits real and imagined, and then look forward to bedding the woman of his choice.

Sometimes all he wanted was a compliant woman who knew his needs. At other times he needed and craved one of the young fillies newly captured. They took some breaking in and he used them to vent his passions on and rid himself of aggression.

Those were the times when their very frailty and their obvious defiance combined to bring out the slumbering violence within him.

Now was one of those nights. He thought of the girl who got away and his anger was such that he must take revenge on her loss by seeking out the girl, little more than a child, he'd taken a couple of nights ago from another burning wagon.

He thought of this quivering girl, with the long blonde hair and the immature body and he wanted to feel her warmth before squeezing and choking her slim white neck. . . .

He hawked and spat and Zac, lolling nearby, moved.

'Hey, Barnaby, mind what you're doin', I don't like bein' spat on!'

'Since when have you been so particular?'

'As of now, buddy. Ma woman just cleaned up ma duds and she'll play hell iffen I even roll in the dirt!'

'Goin' soft, Zac? Give her a whippin' if she get lippy. That's the way to treat women. Spit on her if you has to!'

'Huh! I don' aim to start another war, Barnaby. I likes a quiet life.' He reached for the earthenware demijohn and took another plug of beer, then wiped his lips. 'This woman's a good 'un and I don't want anythin' to happen to her, like what happened to Mary.'

Both men thought of Mary who'd been a virago and Zac had had to knock her out before he could bed her. Zac hadn't called it rape each time he took her but everyone in the camp had known what was happening after her screams had stopped and the silence said it all.

One night in a temper, Zac had shot her. They'd buried her well away from the camp and none of the women had referred to her again.

Barnaby looked at Zac. 'Mary bothers you?'

'Yeh, I seen her ghost.' Zac looked uncomfortable as if Barnaby would laugh at him. Barnaby didn't.

'How long's this been' goin' on?'

Zac shrugged. 'Ever since I buried her.'

'D'you see her?'

'Sometimes. Mostly I hear her.' He shuddered. 'She'll get me some day.' He hiccupped.

'You really believe that? Go on, you're drunk! She might haunt but she can't harm you, for Christ's sake!'

Zac looked at him strangely.

'There's more mysterious things in heaven and on earth than you know about, Barnaby. Mebbe you'll find out some day!'

With that he stood up with some difficulty, staggered away to pee in the bushes, then he made his way to his own cabin.

Barnaby ruminated. Zac was a queer cuss. Sometimes he saw a light in his eyes he didn't like. A kind of challenging light as if he might some day take over the camp. . . . He must watch Zac, and yet it was rumoured he was once a preacher. Would an ex-preacher plot to murder his leader?

Just then in the far woods came a sound to freeze his blood. It was the low distant wailing of a wolf. Or was it a wolf? Zac's talk about haunting had sharpened his imagination. One of the other men half asleep around the fire raised a drunken face and opened an eye.

'Wolves on the prowl tonight, boss? Mebbe we should go have a wolf hunt?'

Barnaby shook his head. 'Go back to sleep, Pete. Nobody goes huntin' at night.'

The sound came again and this time there was a

variation. There was a definite triumphant whoop to it as if the victim had been killed.

Barnaby sat up with a jerk. Hell! That sounded damn well like an Apache yell! Christ! It had been years since he'd heard that particular cry but it still put chills up his back.

What in tarnation was going on?

Then incredibly, the drum began to beat. It came slow and deliberate, each boom resounding as it vibrated, sending out a death message for all those who would hear it.

Barnaby sprang to his feet and kicked a lethargic Pete.

'Get up, you lazy bastard and rouse the boys! Somethin's goin' on down the mountain. Can't you hear it?'

Then came the faint sound of chanting amidst the boom of the drum. The men roused, some coming from the cabins in just their underpants and vests to find out what was happening.

They all looked to Barnaby for an explanation.

'What is it, boss? Are the Indians uprisin'?' someone called.

'How the hell do I know?' he snapped. 'But I'm gonna find out!' He started for the look-out point and cursed their laxness in not having a nighthawk to watch out for danger every night. They'd become far too slack and confident. They only had the Carradines to worry about and the old hermit feller who lived alone and none of them was a real threat.

Now he cursed. The Apache had not risen in these parts for years. Now he wondered the why and the wherefore and were they the Apache target. Maybe they wanted women. . . .

The men crowded around him. The women and the young boys he sent back to their quarters. This was men's business.

'We go and take a look. Take plenty of ammo, boys, and if they're a war-party we'll give 'em a surprise. Right?'

The men let out a roar, keen to have them some excitement. All were criminals and wanted men and sometimes the quiet living and remoteness of their hideout was too much to bear. Tonight maybe there would be some killing and they could get rid of their blood lust.

They moved warily down the mountain, fanning out as they went towards the sound and then as they breasted a small rise they saw the fire and the smoke going up into the night sky. The flicker of flames was intermittent for it was coming from some far glade.

As they cautiously came closer they could smell the smoke and the fire was larger than expected. There was no smell of meat roasting just the smell of green pine which gave off more smoke than dry dead wood, which was curious indeed. Not many Indians made a fire with green wood unless it was for blanket talk, but this could not be because the fire was in a hollow.

They crept on, senses alert and guns at the ready.

The chanting had stopped. The silence hung in the air and the nocturnal animals were still. It was as if the forest was holding its breath and waiting. Waiting for what?

Then Zac, who was with Barnaby, gasped as the wailing came from the north. But now it was not the lonely wail of a hunting wolf but the shriek of an Indian war-whoop. It froze the blood.

'Jesus! Mother of God!' Zac quavered. 'I thought it was Mary! It's those goddamn Apache!'

'Pull yourself together, Zac. Whatever it is, it's human and what's human can be shot!'

The sound came again and this time it was from the south. The men bunched together, uneasy and not liking it.

Pete let off a shot into the bushes and Barnaby grabbed his arm.

'Don't be a fool! Whoever's out there playing darned fool games will know where we are! Have you gone loco!'

Pete was shivering. 'I don't like it. There's no one round that damned fire. I think it's a ghost fire!'

Zac's face blanched. 'Chre-ist! God help me! It's Mary! She's come back with a bunch of demons! She's gonna kill me!' And with that, he turned and ran towards the distant fire, shooting his gun as he went.

Barnaby cursed. If there were enemies out there, they sure knew where they were now. He raised his rifle and taking aim, shot the fleeing man in the back. Zac stumbled and then plunged forward, a crimson stain on his back, before crumpling face down on the ground.

Barnaby ran to him, saw he was still twitching. He looked down coldly at his erstwhile friend. The sight did not disturb him. It served Zac right for panicking. Bloody ghosts indeed!

Pete ran nervously to them both. 'Is he dead?'

Barnaby looked at him and snarled, 'As good as. If you or anyone else here wants to go shootin' their guns off, you'll all get the same! Now git out there and see what's goin' on!'

The sounds came again but this time from the west. Barnaby swung round. This time there was chanting with the sound of the drum thrown in for good measure. The fierce Apache war-cry ululated eerily, icing the blood of those who listened.

'Damn it all to hell! We're surrounded!' Suddenly he too was filled with panic. 'If you're out there, show yorselves, God rot y'all!' but he had the sense not to use his weapon.

Pete plucked at Barnaby's sleeve. 'Give the order, Barnaby. Let's go back and fort-up. These bastards can't go on like this much longer. They're goin' to pick us off one by one if we don't.'

'It's a trick of some kind,' grated Barnaby. 'Not a shot fired, not a flicker of anyone. It's uncanny. But it's a war-chant, all right. I've heard many such chants. They're figurin' on doin' somethin' special.'

'Like what?' asked Pete. 'Sneakin' in and takin' our women?'

He said it half-heartedly and was surprised when Barnaby caught his arm in a vice-like grip.

'The women! Why didn't I think of it? This is a bloody diversion! The sumbitches are playin' with us while they sneak off with the women!'

'They cain't do that, there's only the one way in. We would have seen a band of Indians makin' for the gap!'

Barnaby looked at Pete with contempt. 'If them sons of bitches can hoodwink us, they can get into our valley! Come on, let's get back and see what's goin' on!'

Barnaby shouted his orders and explained his fears.

'This business lured us away from their real intent. Maybe those squaws got a message out to them! I'll have their hides! Come on, boys, hit the breeze and let's get at 'em!'

All was quiet in the camp. The men searched all the cabins. There was not one woman or child to be found.

'I knew it!' raged Barnaby. 'They must have come in over the mountains! Spread out, boys and let's find their tracks!'

Dawn was breaking before they assembled together, shaking their heads. They'd followed tracks from behind the cabins but lost them in the stream that flowed through the valley into the pasture beyond. From there the trample of horses and the small herd of cows they owned had obliterated the rest. It was as if fifteen women and seven children had disappeared from the face of the earth.

Hank Bodell grumbled mightily as he followed Jake and Linx towards the high plateau near their camp to watch for the greatest herd Linx had ever seen.

Linx and Paddy had entered their camp quietly during the night, frightening the shit out of Jake and himself. They'd looked the worse for wear and hungry enough to eat an ox.

The fire had been rekindled and while Jake prepared hot grub, Linx had told them what was happening and why he needed their help.

Charlie lay beside them quiet and still, his wound was healing but he still looked white and drawn.

'So you want us to watch out for this herd you've seen and set 'em stampedin' up the mountain?'

'Yeh. It won't be the whole herd. They was mixed bands that come together once in a while so, the old man says, but we caught us part of a herd and the rest of 'em will be moseyin' around lookin' for 'em. They're the ones who'll be comin' at a gallop.'

'Mmm, you're sure about this?'

'No, of course I'm not sure, dammit! But that old geezer seems to know his herd. They're run by that palomino we was chasin'. Remember him?'

Hank's eyes gleamed. 'I'd like to catch that stallion. He'd be worth a fortune.'

'Yeh, well, it's hands off that 'un. The old man won't play along if he thinks we'll capture his herd. They're his babies.'

'He sounds a queer cuss to me.'

'Yeh, well, he's a white Indian. Been alone too long I guess. But there'll be plenty of mustangs, boss, believe me. We don't need to go hellbent over these here mountains to get our quota. In fact, if we build a good strong corral we can get us enough stock to come back for. How about it?'

Hank looked at him contemplatively. 'You're talkin' mustangs. What about these here Dougans?'

'Like I said, once they're gone, it'll be a doddle.'

Hank scratched his chin. 'It doesn't bother you, wastin' this Dougan bunch?'

'Hell, Hank, we did it durin' the war! This is war of a kind. The whole bloody bunch are desperadoes. Look what we're doin' for the women, we're freein' them!'

'Sounds like out of the fryin' pan inter the fire if they get took by the Carradines.'

Linx shrugged. 'They'll get their chance to stay with them or come away with us. There's more of us than the Carradines. They'll havta play along.'

'Well, it's yor show, Linx. We'd better get started.'

'I'll come too,' Charlie said and stood up stiffly.

'There's no need for you, Charlie. You can look after our camp.'

'If you're goin', boss, then I shall. I can roust mustangs and every pair of lungs will be needed.'

Hank and Linx laughed. They knew the effect of Charlie's deep bellow on frightened mustangs.

So now they were riding to the high plateau to wait and watch. Linx had explained about the Carradines making for the corral of captured horses to be freed to muster with the rest of their herd. The Carradine brothers were then to gather on each side of the gap leading upwards to the forted-up camp in the high valley in the mountains, to close the gap when the mustangs stampeded through into the luscious verdant pasture of that valley.

With luck, the maddened animals would storm the camp, galloping through and flattening the flimsy cabins as they went. Only the log cabins would remain standing, everything else would be pounded to matchwood. All the bronc-busters had witnessed such devastation in the past. It would be like a whirlwind sweeping the ground clean, even low trees could be snapped like twigs.

Hank's leg pained him still, but now he could ride. He could still throw a stick of dynamite along with Jake and follow the panicking herd. Suddenly he was conscious of a rising of his blood. He'd had the same feeling during the war when they were waiting for the Yankees during the calm before the battle commenced.

He let out the Rebel yell and Jake grinned at him. He knew the feeling well.

They reached the plateau as the first streaks of a

new day appeared in the east. Hank sucked in his breath, for far down below was a dark mass that heaved and rippled, like a calm lake with underwater currents. Christ! Linx was right! There they were, a multi-coloured mass of animals quietly grazing, their colours showing more every minute as the light grew stronger.

They made up the largest herd that Hank Bodell had ever seen in his years of hunting mustangs.

To the right of the great herd, he saw through his glasses a breakaway band of horses, making for the higher ground. Yes, that was the bunch the old man was interested in. Then it struck Hank that it must have been the hermit who had shot him in the first place. So he didn't owe that old bastard any favours!

'I'll take that palomino stallion if I get the chance and to hell with the old sonofabitch!' he muttered aloud.

Then it was all go. Two distant shots echoed around the mountains. Hank saw the feeding herd lift their heads as one and begin to move. They started to run and then changed course as another smaller band, which Hank guessed had been those already caught, lured them further up the mountainside.

Jake dug his heels into his horse and spurred ahead.

'Come on, boss, let's get at 'em!'

They moved with breakneck speed down the incline, amidst small boulders, sagebrush and loose scree to the valley bottom where they fanned out, driving the startled mustangs up the winding trail which led to the Dougan Gap. Hank lit a stick of dynamite and hurled it to the far left as Jake did the same on the right. The explosions and puffs of black smoke sent the animals careering ahead, out-distancing the men following behind.

Hank leaned back on his horse pulling on his horse, his leg paining him badly now. He was grinning and waving to Jake and Charlie.

'We've done our bit, boys, it's up to the others now. Let's make for the gap and wait and see what happens!'

Linx, with Abe and Ned watched the main herd join up with the freed mustangs and saw how they were turned to run. He was satisfied. The old man had been right. The old codger had known how his herd would regroup.

He knew Elijah Joe, Billie and Paddy were on the right flank and would be ready to direct the herd if it deviated from the trail.

Then the pounding of hooves became louder. It was like a long roll of thunder and the ground vibrated. Linx climbed up on to a boulder and watched the oncoming herd, his heart in his mouth. He'd never seen such a glorious pounding mass of animals, ever. They came snorting, heads up, tails flying, sleek bodies glistening in the sun's early morning rays. They were a joy to behold.

They jostled and raced, and behind them came the faint echoes of the explosions.

They swept upwards, like a winding snake of many colours as they charged up the trail, a tightly packed bunch which must have counted more than two hundred, Linx estimated.

Then as the leaders wavered as if to scramble upwards amongst the boulders, Linx brought himself back to the business in hand. He let off a couple of shots as did the others, then they were racing alongside the leaders, chivvying them into the gap and only drew rein as the beasts thundered by into the narrow neck of the valley.

It was done. The rest of the herd would follow the leaders to hell.

Far below, he saw the Carradines waiting to close the gap with brushwood when the last of the herd had passed inside.

Linx wondered what the reactions of Barnaby Dougan and his bunch of cut-throats would be.

EIGHT

Sarah sat huddled in a deep cleft in the rocks. Years gone by it had been a stream, draining water from the mountains, but now, dank and with the ground underfoot still muddy after rain, it was waterless after a shift in the earth's crust during a long-gone earthquake.

There was a faint light coming from far beyond and the wind blew through this shaft through the rock. It had been a secret place of the Apache, starting high on the mountainside in the green valley which Dougan and his men had taken over for themselves, a place which those men had never known existed, not being explorers of the valley they chose to hide in.

But the Carradines had known of its existence ever since their father had chased a deer into the outer opening and followed the trail to come and stand and look down into the valley of the Dougans.

Now, Sarah sat surrounded by the womenfolk and the children of the encampment. Tucker

Carradine had insisted she go to give the women the courage to leave with them.

They had packed up and followed willingly when Sarah talked to them. Some feared vengeance from their menfolk if caught. Sarah assured them if they would only trust and have patience, they would be united with their families as soon as the danger was past.

Tucker listened to Sarah's impassioned speech. He laughed inwardly. Sarah was making a good impression, but there would be no going back to their kinfolk. They would all be staying with the Carradines and woe betide any of them who tried to escape!

He would have Sarah for himself. She was a spirited filly and it would be amusing to bring her to heel. Those too old or uncomely would become slaves for Ma. That should please the old besom and keep her off his back. As for Tilly . . . he wondered if the young Irishman would take her off their hands. Tilly had an eye for him.

Their instructions had been abrupt and to the point.

'Don't leave this place. You are safe here, but outside is danger from both men and wild beasts, so stay where you are!'

It would be easy to herd them back again along the passage and back into their valley. This time they wouldn't have the Dougans as masters but the Carradines!

Meanwhile, Tucker and the rest would have to get out there and wait by Dougan's Gap and be ready to lock in the coming herd.

Tucker looked forward to gaining a goodly herd of mustangs nearly as much as acquiring a harem of women. He would also take the broken-in horses of the bronc-busters. Nobody around these parts would miss a bunch of bronc-busters. . . .

He dreamed as they made their way to the Gap.

It was the first time Barnaby Dougan had faced an irate mob.

'Now hold it, fellers, no need to take that tone with me! I've led you good and proper all these years and now just because somethin' unforeseen happens you want to lynch me!' He levelled his gun at Pete and a big man called Rocky. 'The first man who rushes me and you two get it!'

Pete glanced nervously at the men beside him. 'Steady on boys. The boss is right. He's always looked after us and we can't blame him for what's happened. Women and kids don't just disappear inter thin air. There must be an explanation.' The boys began to mutter. It sounded like the growl of a hungry beast.

'We want our women and kids,' one man bawled. 'How do we know they're still alive?'

Barnaby moved uneasily. He hadn't thought of that explanation. But that was ridiculous. There would have been signs of a massacre, blood and such and where could the bodies have been thrown? The river wasn't deep enough or fast enough to hide all signs of them. He looked around the valley. The dawn was breaking and the silhouettes of the mountains stood out sharp and clear.

'They're here somewhere,' he grated. 'We'll eat and spread out again and this time we comb every gully and creek and cave. We must come up with something!'

Then it came, the faint vibration of the ground and the distant roar as of thunder. Barnaby looked at the sky. There was no sign of rain.

'A storm brewing up,' Pete opined. He, too, was watching the sky.

'Or an earthquake,' Rocky muttered. 'I don't like it! It's not thunder and it's actin' queer for an earthquake.'

The roaring grew louder. It reminded Barnaby of a cavalry charge during the war. It made his belly turn to water, bringing back distant memories of being overrun by General Grant's men during the last assault at Petersburg when it was every man for himself.

The men beside Barnaby began to panic.

'Hold it, boys, them's hosses comin' up the trail. I'll bet my last dollar on it! No need to worry, boys, we can handle a few hosses!' He laughed, relieved at the explanation. A stampeding herd was a damn sight better than a bloody earthquake! 'Come on, let's catch us some hosses!'

They mounted up and rode towards the gap, splitting the bunch into two parts with the intention of closing the gap when the wild horses galloped into the valley.

Barnaby breathed a sigh of relief. This interlude would take the men's minds off the women and kids for a spell.

They watched as the leaders, foaming at the mouth and covered in froth and sweat streamed through the opening, heads up, manes and tails flying. It looked as if all the demons of hell were after them.

Barnaby cheered and the men took up the cry. Soon, they would have themselves a goodly remuda of horses to break in.

Then as the stream of horses became never ending, Barnaby began to be afraid.

As the horses galloped through the narrow gap they fanned out, kicking their heels up and racing ever onwards like animals who were running blind.

'What is this?' Barnaby yelled. 'What in hell's got into the bastards?'

He waited for no answer but yanked his horse around and galloped in front of the ever-growing horde of sweating snorting animals.

He was aware of the rest of his men racing beside him, as the thunder of hooves came nearer and nearer behind him.

For the first time it occurred to him that his horse would be outrun. A horse without a rider was much faster. . . . His heart took a leap. Jesus Christ! A hoof in a rabbit hole and he would be a gonner. Fear hit him and he was conscious of a hot wetness soaking his saddle. . . .

The wild mustangs came on, wave after wave, spreading out and blindly galloping into and over everything in their way. Barnaby heard shrieks and yells and the dull thuds of beasts hitting fences and flimsy lean-to shelters. There was the splintering of wood and the screams of yearlings as they crashed and fell before the onslaught of others. The wave of fear was maddening the herd and the spilled blood was sending them crazy.

Barnaby fell off his tottering horse in front of his cabin. It was stoutly built and he dived inside, cursing. Rocky and a couple of other riders hurtled inside too before he crashed the door closed and bolted it with the stout wooden plank.

It was dark inside for the windows were small. Barnaby could hear the laboured breathing and the stink of fear on them all. It took a while before he could calm himself enough to speak.

'Anyone else alive out there?'

'I saw Pete trampled underfoot and Wall-Eye copped it,' Rocky said in a grating whisper. 'I don't know about the rest.'

'Antonio disappeared into the first bunch that came through,' another man muttered.

'Goddammit!' raged Barnaby. 'How the hell do we get out of this lot?'

'We sit it out,' Rocky said calmly. 'It looks mighty like someone set the critters stampedin' up this way kinda deliberate!'

'You mean those Carradines? They haven't the brains!'

'No, but them there bronc-busters do! They know how mustangs react and come together!' Barnaby and Rocky stared at each other in the dimness of the cabin. Barnaby cursed.

'Those sons of bitches, the Carradines are to blame! We should have killed the lot of them years ago! You and Pete stopped me . . .'

'Hold hard, boss. You yourself said they was useful, layin' traps and such. They was dumb. It was a long time before they cottoned on to us stealin' their meat!'

'Yeh, well, look where it's got us. Listen to them goddamned beasts!' The pandemonium outside grew to a crescendo orchestrated with mighty crashes on the stout walls as panicked animals galloped headlong into unseen barriers.

The pine-logged walls shivered but held. They could hear amidst the din the lowing of cattle as their own herd was sucked into the jumble of bodies.

Then after what seemed hours and hours the noise became less and the onslaught of maddened beasts on the cabin stopped. Barnaby ventured to open the door and take a look. He was appalled at the sight.

The door was hard to open for a mustang with a broken neck lay alongside it and all along the front of the cabin was a piled-up mass of bodies of both horses and steers.

'Jesus!' he gasped and closed the door quickly as he watched the tail end of the herd gallop more slowly by. They were the yearlings and the mares with foals and they were following their instincts and tagging along behind. 'The whole bloody valley is a mass of horses and they're circlin' around, and outside there, we've got a bloody wall of dead 'uns!

'We'll just havta stick it out,' Rocky grunted. 'We got water and grub.'

'Not much, we ain't! Less than a bucket of water and the grub for the camp was kept in the shack near the fire. The women wanted it that way so's we all got fair shares!' answered Barnaby.

'Then we'll havta tighten our belts and hope these bastards eat all the grass and move out.'

'Not if they was sent in deliberate!'

There was utter silence as all the men digested what it would mean. It could come to a siege!

Barnaby licked his lips. He was a hard man when he was dealing with frightened helpless victims but now . . . this was different. This was a matter of his life or death and his guts turned to water.

Let's make a break for it now!'

'We can't! It's full daylight and they'll shoot us down!'

'If they're out there! Maybe they're not. Who'd

risk their lives amongst those hosses?'

In a frenzy, Barnaby pulled the door open. A stream of daylight came in blinding them all. He put a hand up to shade his eyes and stepped over the carcass with a sense of swagger. He'd show the bastards even though he was shitting himself!

A shot came, a bullet twanged only inches from his head and he ducked inside and slammed the door. He breathed deeply.

'So they risked comin' in with the hosses.' Rocky sounded mocking as he loaded up his guns as did the other two silent men. Barnaby did likewise.

Rocky broke the pane of glass from the small window at the right of the door and Barnaby did the same on the left. The two men went to the rear, opened the back door, then pulled a bedstead across the opening and stuffed a mattress against it as protection. They crouched low and waited.

Then the firing began in earnest.

Outside, Linx and his men had come pounding in behind the herd. They'd seen the carnage, the dead men trampled into bloody pieces of meat, the flimsy shelters collapsing like houses of cards. Awed, they'd followed through until they'd come to the one standing cabin. They'd watched, not knowing whether anyone had escaped inside.

Barnaby's opening the door and stepping out had been the answer. They'd recognized the big man. They'd got him like a rat in a trap!

Linx laughed as his shot sent Barnaby scurrying

inside. Let the bastard stew, they'd get him in the end!

They still did not know just how many were holed up. It didn't matter anyway. They'd pick 'em all off in the end.

'Right, boys, let's give 'em a salvo like we did in the war!' and they let fly, hearing glass tinkle and the thud of bullets splintering wood.

There were two gunmen, one firing from each tiny window. Then Abe gave a yell. There was a man running hell for leather from the back, ducking and dodging across the yard. Abe took his time, allowing the man to run and feel triumphant that he'd got away unnoticed. Then aiming for his back, he fired. The man threw up his arms, a red stain spreading and he catapulted forward to lie outstretched on the ground.

Abe turned away and watched the back door for any other hopeful. None came.

Linx wiped his brow.

'We're gettin' nowhere,' he growled. 'We're just wastin' bullets. We'll fire the bloody cabin and burn 'em out!'

Jake grunted. 'I've still got a stick of dynamite. We'll let 'em have it.'

'A good idea, Jake. Let's do it!'

The firing ceased and Barnaby and Rocky looked at each other. The third man was shivering as with an ague. He'd watched his buddy die. There but for the grace of God, he could have been the one. They'd tossed for the one to go first. He'd lost and watched his pal lose the gamble.

Now he faced the others.

'I don't like it! They're playin' with us!'

'Pull yorself together, Skitter, they mebbe wanna talk.'

Skitter's teeth chattered. 'I don't wanna die!' His words ended in a scream. Barnaby's fist in his face stopped him abruptly.

'Why, you no-good yeller-livered rat just get out there and talk to them assholes. Here, take this,' and he shoved a nearly white kerchief into his hand. 'Wave it as you go and tell whoever's out there that we come out, no tricks. You understand?'

Skitter stared at him.

'I cain't do it! I cain't face 'em. Don't make me!' He began to shake and sob.

Barnaby spat on the floor. He smiled.

'Right then, sonny, you don't havta do it!'

'I don't?' The relief on Skitter's face brought a look of contempt on Rocky's. It did not change as Barnaby shot Skitter through the throat. He spat on the floor.

'So, there's only you and me, Barnaby,' He towed Skitter to one side. 'Now what do we do?'

'Wait and see what they want.'

The firing started again but this time it was not aimed at the windows. It was as if those out there were playing games. Smoke filled the air outside and it was difficult to see. Their enemies had been elusive like ghosts. Barnaby thought of Pete and his dread of the supernatural. It was getting to him and he fought off the urge to rush outside firing as he went. It was going to take all their survival techniques to see another dawn.

Then suddenly something came hurtling down the stone chimney and rolled on to the hearth. Smoke wisped upwards and out and the two men turned, aghast at what they saw . . . the thick cigar-shaped object . . . Barnaby shit his pants.

Then the boom came, and the belching forth of orange-red flames and the smoke. Barnaby's last thought was that he had been catapulted into Hell.

The Carradines watched from afar as the cabin blew up. They cheered and Tilly danced around and Ma, with lips folded in disapproval looked at the herd of horses, more concerned with them than the passing of the Dougan bunch.

They made their way down into the valley clumsily, Tilly slipping and sliding down on her backside in her hurry to find the men. She wanted Paddy and now Ma must allow her to have her way.

They found Linx and the rest of the broncbusters waiting for them.

'Hi! You did a good job,' Linx called as they approached.

'The next thing is to go to the womenfolk and guide them out of the mountain. Tucker, you go with us and we'll leave your brothers to cut out as many mustangs as you can manage and get 'em corralled away from the rest. Meanwhile, ma'am,' turning to Ma Carradine, 'perhaps you and your daughter could prepare some grub? We have coffee and the makin's with us.'

Tilly sidled forward. 'Could he stay behind?' She pointed to Paddy. 'We need help in carrying water and findin' fresh kindlin'.'

'Tilly!' barked Ma, 'we can do all that. Now let the menfolk get on with their own business!' She cuffed Tilly.

'Ma! It's not fair!'

Ma slapped her again. 'Fair or not, you're doin' what I say or I'll blister that hot arse of yors!'

Paddy turned away, grinning. He wondered what it would be like to have Tilly under him, not that he fancied her, his mind was on Sarah, but if it was offered on a plate, who in his right mind would refuse such a dish?

Tucker Carradine led the way to the dry creek entrance. It looked to be a small cave that might have been the lair for some wild beast. It was well hidden. A rider could pass by many times and not notice it.

But once inside, the crack widened and from far above there came a faint beam of light, which meant the crack had been split in some long distant past. The walls were smooth and the ground gravelled and sandy. Linx ran his hands over the walls and realized that over millions of years the water-course had ground a way through the splits in the rock to make a gully that once was a torrent of water filtered through from the mountain. Now it only ran water after the winter melt.

They groped their way through the tunnel, sometimes ducking low and at other times the ceiling was high and a fresh breeze came through and cut like a knife. At last the tunnel widened into a small cavern. There were stalactites and the faint sound of dripping water hit the ears. Crouched close together for warmth and courage were the huddled womenfolk hugging their children close. They looked apprehensive as they approached.

Sarah stood up stiffly.

'Thank God, you're here, I . . . been a long time and we're so cold!' She shivered.

Linx looked at the other women – all looked white and pinched and he saw the despair in their eyes as they clutched their children to them. The babies slept, swathed in shawls, the older children snivelled quietly.

'Come,' he said, 'we'll take you back. Ma Carradine is preparing food and coffee. Then we'll take you away and you can all join our camp and we'll get you back to yor kinfolk.'

One of the women struggled to her feet.

'What about those who have no kinfolk? Some of us would be ashamed to go back!'

Linx blinked. He hadn't thought of that kind of

situation. Tucker Carradine thrust him out of the way.

'Any of you ladies who choose to stay can stay with us under our protection.' He smiled at them all. Inside, he was assessing them. Not one of them would escape. . . .

The speaker looked at the other women.

'Any of you take up this man's offer?'

There were mutterings and then another took courage and spoke up for the rest.

'We prefer to go out of these goddamned mountains. We want to settle in a town and give our kids a chance!'

Linx shrugged. 'The choice is yors, ma'am. We'll escort you wherever you want to go.'

It was a weary bunch who gathered by Ma Carradine's fire and ate the frugal grub and drank the hot coffee.

It was then that Tucker Carradine and his brothers struck.

Linx and his men were lounging aound the fire when it happened. Billie, being the youngest of them had been despatched to the river to bring water and as he returned with two full buckets he saw the little drama unfold.

The Carradines surrounded the lounging men. Billie dropped his buckets when he heard the gun triggers being cocked. Hell! What was going on?

Tucker swaggered in front of Linx and his men, enjoying the importance of the occasion. He not only wanted to savour it, but to show his doubting ma that he could plan a course of action and carry it out.

'The womenfolk ain't goin' back, Linx Firman. They stay here with us. Any objections?'

Linx looked at him coolly, shoving his hat well back off his forehead.

'You must be jokin' Tucker! You don't need 'em all! How would you control 'em? They're not a bunch of cows you can corral.'

Tucker moved uneasily.

'There's Bill and Jed and those we don't need can help Ma. They can do the work.'

'You're outa yor mind, mister. You cain't run 'em all.'

'We say we can. Bill and Jed agree.' Tucker was getting angry now. He was conscious of his ma standing by, disapproving. He looked at her helplessly. 'You want women in the camp, don't you, ma?'

Ma Carradine did not answer. Tilly looked at her brother defiantly.

'Iffen you lot have women then I wanna man!'

'Tilly!' and Ma's voice was a roar. 'When I get a hold on you I'll tan yor hide!'

Billie crept closer to listen. His heart thumped. He felt for the gun Elijah Joe had given him. It seemed a long time ago. If he could get off a shot to frighten Tucker, then it would give Linx and the others a chance to do something.

It was Luke who started the action. He ran across

the open space, an unearthly figure in the flickering light.

'Ma! There's a feller in the bushes!' Every eye turned towards him. Billie panicked and his shot caught the idiot boy in the back of the head. He sprawled on the ground and as Billie stared at him, paralysed with shock at what he had done, Tucker's bullet took him in the forehead.

The womenfolk screamed as Linx grabbed his gun and splatted two shots into Tucker Carradine. Then Ma's gravelly voice stopped the sudden mayhem as the Carradine brothers aimed at Ned and Abe and the others.

'Stop it, you bastards! I want no more killin', d'you hear?' She ran forward and stood with arms outstretched between them all. 'Goddammit! There's been enough bloodshed around here! Let it be! I don't want any damned women around here! Leave us, alone and get to hell out of it! Go on, just go and may you all rot in hell!' She sank down to her knees and cradled Tucker's head in her arms. 'Poor stupid Tucker who thought he was so smart!'

Linx looked with pity at the old woman who showed such bitterness and despair. Then he turned to the others.

'We'll havta make a camp for the womenfolk, Ned, Elijah Joe, you're a woodsman, show 'em how to make a temporary Indian shelter while we see to Billie.' He looked at Ma Carradine. 'We'll help you folk dig graves if you want?'

She gave him a hard stare.

'We bury our own,' she said and turned her back on him.

Hank Bodell and his partner, Linxlater Firman often retold the saga of the best most profitable round-up of wild mustangs they'd ever had. They fired many an up-and-coming would-be bronc-buster with the tale of the mighty herd of animals they'd witnessed up in the Montana mountain ranges, but they never referred to the Carradines or the massacre of the Dougan gang or the womenfolk and their offspring they had saved who'd scattered and settled in towns close by.

Hank never spoke of his mistake in shooting Sarah Crayshaw. He told her long years afterwards that he was to blame. She smiled and patted his arm and kissed him lightly on the cheek.

'It's in the past, Hank. If it wasn't for you and the boys I shouldn't be here now.'

They were sitting on the veranda of Paddy and Sarah O'Rourke's ranch house watching the sun go down. Hank and Linx visited with them each time they were in the vicinity.

They would talk about the past and the two men would take a walk to Paddy's corrals and look over the horses that Paddy had made famous over the years. An O'Rourke horse was prized, well broken in and ready to ride.

They also eyed those with the old palomino stallion's characteristics: the rare throwbacks with the glowing golden-brown coats and the cream manes and tails. But they knew Paddy wouldn't sell those very special animals. They were the nucleus of his new herd.

They would also go and visit Elijah Joe, now living quietly on part of Paddy's spread. Hank now knew that it had been Elijah Joe who'd taken a pot-shot at him and even now his thigh still throbbed and ached after too much riding. He held no grudge. It was all in the past as Sarah pointed out.

They would talk about the past and if Elijah Joe was in the mood, they would ride up the mountain and visit the old soddy where Elijah Joe had lived alone except for his wolf for so many years.

Hank noticed how the old man wandered to the mound that was Trapper's grave and came away looking melancholy. Then he would go and stand at his look-out and stare at the breathtaking view before sighing and coming back to them.

'Ah well,' he would mutter, 'it was a long time ago.' Then he would smile and fill his old pipe. 'You know what? One of these days I'll get Paddy and his boys to round up that old stallion and bring him in with a couple of his old mares to keep him company and I'll make sure he's cared for, for the rest of his life.'

'Why don't you do it now, Elijah Joe?'

Elijah Joe grimaced. 'I want him to be free as long as he can enjoy his freedom. It's no fun growing old and bein' corralled. I know that,' he said wistfully. 'There's a whole lot of range I've never travelled and I wish I had, but it's too late for me. The stallion's different. He's still gotta life. When he hasn't, then I'll take care of him.'

Hank and Linx would smile and shake their heads and they would go away and plan their next round-up. Life had to go on.